"Are you okay?"

"I'm fine but you're heavy. I need to breathe."

"Don't move from where you are. The seat's low enough you're covered by the front frame of the car. Keep your head down and as low to the dash as you can. I want to check out what's going on."

Hard, unflinching cop lined each and every word that fell from his lips, including the fact that he'd given an order he had every expectation would be obeyed.

But what had happened?

Was this a random act? Marlowe lived in a large metropolitan area and knew it wasn't only possible, but it happened to people every day.

Yet even as she considered it, with the sounds of shouts outside the car a steady accompaniment to her lying in wait for Wyatt's all clear, she couldn't help but wonder if that was delusional thinking designed to make herself feel better.

Wyatt was working on a major case.

Was it possible this shooting was tied into that and not really random at all?

And if it was, what had Wyatt actually uncovered on the bottom of the harbor?

Dear Reader,

Welcome to the first book in my new series, New York Harbor Patrol. This book has been such a joy to write, and I'm incredibly excited to craft this series of romantic and suspensefully imagined stories about the lives of the people who work in New York, protecting the city from dangers in the water.

In the first book we meet Detective Wyatt Trumball, a scuba diver for the police. He's working an incredibly challenging case and discovers three small safes, each attached to kayakers who were mysteriously murdered in the waters around New York City. The civilian partner helping him out? Marlowe McCoy, one of the best safecrackers in New York.

As a New Yorker myself, I find it hard to describe just how present water is as a dimension of living in the city. I love visiting Governors Island, walking the Brooklyn Bridge or staring out over the Hudson on a weekend jaunt around town.

I hope you enjoy this first story about those who make their living protecting the city—their drive and their courage and their insistence on protecting a home they love. Of course, it's not all smooth sailing, especially when there are some surprisingly dangerous things to uncover down in the depths...

Best,

Addison Fox

DANGER IN THE DEPTHS

Addison Fox

HARLEQUIN

ROMANTIC
SUSPENSE

Recycling programs for this product may not exist in your area.

ISBN-13: 978-1-335-59367-2

Danger in the Depths

Copyright © 2023 by Frances Karkosak

Harlequin Enterprises ULC
22 Adelaide St. West, 41st Floor
Toronto, Ontario M5H 4E3, Canada
www.Harlequin.com

Printed in U.S.A.

Addison Fox is a lifelong romance reader, addicted to happily-ever-afters. After discovering she found as much joy writing about romance as she did reading it, she's never looked back. Addison lives in New York with an apartment full of books, a laptop that's rarely out of sight and a wily beagle who keeps her running. You can find her at her home on the web at addisonfox.com or on Facebook (Facebook.com/addisonfoxauthor) and Twitter (@addisonfox).

Visit the Author Profile page at Harlequin.com.

For my new neighbors, Patience and Sam. It's wonderful to know you're around the corner!

Chapter 1

"The whales have really come back for this?"

NYPD Detective Wyatt Trumball stared down into the murky waters of the East River and corrected his dive partner, Gavin Hayes. "They're back in the Atlantic. No self-respecting mammal would touch these waters."

"Except us," Gavin sighed.

"Except us," Wyatt agreed as he fitted his full face mask down into place.

"Why doesn't anyone read the signs?" Officer Amos Yearwood asked. Although he wasn't a diver, Amos was an accomplished swimmer and a valued member of the harbor team patrol. Also dressed in a full dry suit like Wyatt and Gavin, he'd navigate the Zodiac boat as well as their advanced sonar devices while they did the dive, searching for a missing kayaker they'd been called to rescue.

Or find.

"You mean those big ones?" Gavin joked. "The ones that are posted at every point someone can possibly drop into the river?"

Amos only nodded, his gaze continually scanning the waves around them.

The water was running hard today. Despite its name, the East River wasn't actually a river, but a tidal estuary that connected the New York Bay to the Long Island Sound. This particular body of water was a delightful quirk of Mother Nature's design and, as such, changed its direction regularly. She was mean, nasty and more than willing to chew up and spit out those who didn't respect her power.

Hordes of New Yorkers chose to ignore this fact every year. Especially the ones who loved to try and kayak in her waters.

"What's wrong with these people?" Gavin shook his head, scanning the water. "Everyone thinks they're invincible."

Wyatt nodded before fitting his breathing apparatus into place. Everyone did think they were invincible.

Until they weren't.

They'd been called out on the emergency rescue twelve minutes ago and even with the other boats already on patrol in and around Hell Gate, one of the most dangerous confluence points in the river, he had little hope they'd find the kayaker alive.

Which was a hell of a way to start a search and rescue.

Settling himself at the edge of the Zodiac, Wyatt gave one final look to the New York City skyline that rose up in front of him before dropping backward into the water.

Wyatt's entire world changed immediately. The bright, early September sunlight that glazed Manhattan's skyscrapers in gold vanished, the water surrounding him dark, murky and swift. He gave himself a moment to get oriented, that environmental change something he'd not only trained for, but lived with each time he dropped into the water.

He'd learned long ago it was best to give that change its due. To allow the moment to sweep over him, those few precious seconds to reorient himself well worth it before he began his work.

Gavin had already begun to move, the kick up of silt and murky water swirling around Wyatt's face mask.

Amos would keep up steady chatter with them via their comms unit, along with the rest of the harbor team on the surrounding boats. They had a rhythm and a system for working the bottom of the waterway and it was about time they got to it.

Wyatt took the opposite direction as Gavin, his thickly gloved hands moving through the silt of the riverbed as soon as he'd completed his descent. The visibility was minimal, even with the light mounted on his head, and Wyatt kept his movements slow and steady, even as he quickly released handfuls of silt he managed mostly on shape.

Empty bottles, rotting wood, discarded pieces of metal—he'd knocked his shin on an engine once—all lay on the estuary's floor. But it was those things on the floor that he was regularly tasked to find. Evidence retrieval, sweeps for bombs, and search and rescue were all part of the job. And while the twelve-hour shifts were long, they moved at a rapid clip when he was under the water.

A strange counterpoint to actual life underwater, which was quiet and eerie on the best of days.

If life on land was chaos, the water was a strange sort of limbo. A receiving ground for that chaos, even as everything floated and settled when in the water. A murky wasteland for all that people destroyed, eliminated or flat-out wanted to forget.

Wyatt let it drift through the back of his mind, a gentle reminder of why he did what he did.

He knew who he was. And he knew he was driven by a higher purpose, one passed down from father to son.

"Wyatt. I'm getting a signature on something." Amos's voice was crisp and clear in his comms unit. "The heat signature is cooling fast, but I'm getting a read. Fifty feet to your right."

He tapped out a quick response on the wrist unit he wore affirming receipt of the message, then shifted to his right as Amos had directed. He kept up the steady movement over silt, his fingers skimming the river's floor, even though he avoided grasping any fistfuls. This time, his aim was the lingering heat signature. He had no hope of pulling someone out alive, but if they found the lost kayaker, he could retrieve the body and they could wrap this dive.

He moved, slow and steady, in the direction he'd been given, Amos's voice alerting him as he closed in on forty feet, then thirty, and so on. The water flowed around his dry suit, a swirling, raging storm at odds with the calm above.

Damn, the water was churned up today.

It was his last thought as his hand hit something firm and solid, an image filling the hazy space in front of him.

A body, eyes wide open, stared sightlessly toward the surface.

He felt a momentary shot of sadness at the loss of life. A silly, needless waste that could have been avoided if the man had simply selected another route. Had read the posted signs and recognized this wasn't the place he needed to be, no matter how confident he was in his skills.

Wyatt tapped another note to Amos, confirming he'd found the package.

"Damn, Trumball, that was fast. Good work. Let me get Gavin and we'll head your way."

Wyatt tapped his agreement, then went back to his perusal of the body. His headlamp gave off enough light in the murky darkness to make out the long, thin form of the kayaker. As he took in the length of the body, his gaze narrowed on the man's hands. Even now in death, they were wrapped tightly around what looked to be a small safe.

Wyatt reached forward, trying to pull the safe toward him when he realized the man had harnessed himself to the metal, a series of bungee cords wrapped around his midsection. It was odd—what was a kayaker doing with a safe in the middle of the East River?—when Wyatt caught sight of the real problem and the likely cause of death.

They could blame the raging waterway and its six knots of running water this sunny afternoon, but Wyatt would bet his next paycheck that wasn't what killed the guy.

Nope.

That honor likely belonged to the large, gaping hole in his chest, shot through with what looked to be a bullet from a long-range sniper's rifle.

Marlowe McCoy slung the large leather bag that held the tools of her trade over her shoulder and headed into the police station. The sticky, pasted-on heat of August had given way to a gorgeous late summer day of early September and she was happy to be out of the shop for a while.

And this was, after all, the 86th.

She'd been in nearly every precinct in the borough of Brooklyn, but had a lingering fondness for the 86th. Whether it was her grandfather's stories of running wild throughout the neighborhood or the fact that she could feel the history of the place in its dingy walls, she wasn't sure. But she liked it here.

She liked her shop in Park Slope a lot better, but very little police work came to her. And based on the short briefing she'd received a half hour ago, this was a job she most definitely needed to do on site.

Although she had little interest in what lay inside the safes she opened for the cops, she couldn't deny that she was intrigued by the call. A kayaker gone missing in the East River had turned up, physically tied to a small safe. The bomb squad had already done their work over it and she was pretty well guaranteed no surprises on that front.

So now she was up to open the safe in hopes it would

provide some understanding as to what got the guy killed.

"Marlowe!" One of the desk cops called out to her as she crossed over to the security screening required of all guests to the precinct. "You catch that Yankees game last night?"

"You know I'm a Mets girl, Sinclair."

The man—one who'd trained under her grandfather— waved a hand. "Bah. You know that's a perpetual lost cause."

"What can I say. Hope springs eternal." Marlowe grabbed her bag of tricks off the conveyor belt and re-settled the bag over her arm. "But I do wish you luck in the playoffs. New York's a lot more fun in the fall when the playoffs are running in either team's favor."

"That it is." Sinclair nodded his gray head as she passed through. "See you later, darlin'."

Somewhere deep inside, Marlowe knew she should swat him for the "darlin'," but she didn't have the heart. Sinclair had known her since she was small and the ex-pression was one of affection and warmth.

Even if it did come with a bit of license others weren't even remotely entitled to.

"Hey there, Legs." Wyatt Trumball pushed himself off the wall next to the precinct conference room and walked toward her. "Or should I call you Darlin' Safe-cracker?"

He was tall—about six-one to her own five-nine— and he had a lithe, athletic form that always made her look twice.

Damn him.

She had no interest in looking at Wyatt even once,

let alone multiple times, but her traitorous eyes always found a reason to seek him out when she was in his presence. For that very reason, if she could ignore him altogether without being obvious and rude about it she would.

But there was no ignoring Detective Wyatt Trumball. And attempting it would only set him off.

Even if he was insistent in calling her some sort of nickname every time he saw her. Names that should have been insulting and objectifying, but which gave her an unbridled thrill all the same.

Maybe because, odd as it was, they weren't objectifying at all. Not when his dark, sexy voice flowed over her like a warm waterfall.

She was even in carefully selected slacks for the occasion. Forget the fact that her job went easier in her standard uniform of black slacks and button down blouse, but she'd be damned if she'd deliberately wear a skirt or dress in his presence.

He was one of the NYPD's elite. A well-respected detective with the harbor team that worked in and around the waters of New York City, with a specific expertise as a scuba diver. He was good at what he did—rather amazing, actually—but he had an ego to match that never failed to scratch at the edges of her nerves. Even as she fought the frustratingly hot licks of attraction that swirled fast and furious around those edges, too.

The man was six feet plus of muscle, sinew and attitude and if she could bottle it she'd likely make a mint.

Instead, she was forced to work with him too often for comfort.

"This is the second safe you've called me in for in the

past month. It would have been the third if you hadn't made the bad and, might I add, cheap, choice to call in Jasper Middleton. You mining gold on the ocean floor?"

"Shh." He leaned in and whispered against her ear as they stepped into the conference room. "That's the last thing we need getting out. My team pulls too many amateurs out of the water each year as it is. Start letting people think there's treasure to be found and we might as well live in our wet suits."

Marlowe fought the shivers racing up and down her spine at the wash of his breath over her ear and the deeply sexy tone in his voice. She fought for something light and breezy in return and ended up being grateful her words remained steady. "I thought you lived in one already."

"You don't like my uniform?" He stepped back and her eyes did that helpless thing where they followed the lines of his body.

But who could blame her?

The way his large, capable hands moved over his flat stomach, smoothing over the deep navy blue of his NYPD T-shirt. A T-shirt that did nothing to hide the solid chest underneath as well as the firm, flexing biceps visible under the sleeves.

Biceps, she suspected, he was well aware drew attention because when her gaze returned to his liquid blue one it was lit with amusement.

Since arguing would require more looking at him she turned on her heel and headed for the safe laid out on the conference room table. Various evidence bags were set out beside it and two of the officers she knew from Forensics stood sentinel at the end of the table, hands already clad in rubber gloves.

"What do you think, Marlowe?" one of the forensics leads asked, her brow knit. "You think it'll be like the first two?"

"I don't want to assume, but I won't take a bet that you're wrong. Especially since you told me the last safe I opened for you had the same outcome as Jasper's."

"Bomb squad already went over it." The second officer moved closer. "Clean like the last two."

Marlowe considered the safe on the table. Although the police department was careful with what they told her—she was a civilian after all—gossip flowed as strong and steady as hot coffee and the local currents. And this was the third safe pulled out of New York waters in the past four weeks.

If she was going to take bets, she'd take the one that said this safe had come out attached to a body like the first two.

But why?

"Standard issue office safe." She pulled out a few of her tools, leaning over the rectangular safe that had been pulled from the water. It had already been cleaned off and no doubt dusted for fingerprints. As she examined it, she saw little to indicate it had spent time in water or covered in fingerprint dust.

The safe was about a cubic foot in size, big enough to hold papers or cash or whatever else a person wanted to keep secure. The same sort found in hotel rooms the world over.

Only unlike those hotel room safes that could be reprogrammed with a master code, this one was locked up tight. She put through the standard masters she had access to as a lock and vault technician, each one coming up empty. She took out a few of her electronics tools, trying those next.

Still nothing.

While any time spent underwater likely didn't do the electronics mechanism any good, the absolute lack of response made her think of the last safe she'd opened for the cops.

No doubt about it, she thought as she stepped away from the table. It looked like she was going to have to drill to unlock this baby's secrets.

Wyatt watched Marlowe work, slow and steady as a metronome, and wondered why this single woman got under his skin so easily.

She was a nuisance, with her knowing eyes and lush, always-smirking mouth. She walked around his cop shop like she owned it. And, of late, she'd seemed to be underfoot more than usual.

And damn it, he wanted her so badly he was nearly blind with it.

He'd known of her before he'd actually known her. Chief of Detectives Anderson McCoy was a legend in the 86th. And although he'd been before Wyatt's time in the NYPD, he was still a larger-than-life presence in the precinct.

The stories about him were renowned to the point of being nearly mythical. His personal life even more so. The hardworking honest-to-a-fault cop. His only son, the rogue black sheep that regularly spent time with his thievery escapades, detailed in the New York newspapers and beyond. And the wide-eyed granddaughter who'd become Anderson's responsibility when it became evident her father's luck had run out.

Michael McCoy was now a lifelong personal guest of a maximum security prison upstate, a fact that had reportedly nearly destroyed Anderson.

And his granddaughter.

Wyatt took in the tall, slim form of the woman across the room. Slim wasn't quite right, he amended in his mind as he took in the athletic grace that was evident in the firm lines of her arms, the movements of her back and the descent into a tapered waist.

But it was those legs…

He'd never considered himself particularly attracted to any given part of a woman—he liked everything about women—but Marlowe McCoy had a pair of legs that could steal a man's breath. Long, gorgeous and gracefully muscular, the woman could turn heads at a thousand paces.

Although she was always dressed down when she came to the precinct, he'd seen her running often enough through the Park Slope neighborhood they both lived in. She was as fond of Prospect Park as he was and he savored any morning that provided an opportunity to see her on an early run, her legs displayed perfectly beneath her running shorts.

He'd tease her on those mornings, pacing next to her and enjoying the banter that never seemed to progress past fourth grade insults. He'd tried often enough to get her to join him for breakfast after the run but there was always an excuse. An early morning job, a planned visit with her grandfather or, when she wasn't quick enough to come up with an excuse, a flat-out no.

So why did he keep asking?

What was it about Marlowe that intrigued him? Although he loved the thrill of the chase as much as the next guy, he also knew when to leave a woman alone. A fact that had become more and more obvious of late. His last serious girlfriend had been—Wyatt stilled for a moment as the truth washed over him—eighteen months ago already?

Damn.

Nearly two years and he really hadn't been interested in anyone since then.

Anyone except Marlowe.

That truth danced under his thoughts, those mornings when he caught sight of her in the park more exciting and enticing than any night out at the bar.

The woman got to him, in a way that was equal parts breathtaking and terrifying. He didn't do relationships. He might live several hours a day a few hundred feet under the water, but he liked the relationships in his life at surface level, giving no one a chance to dive too deep.

Yeah, sure, it was at odds with his profession. But he'd lost everything once and he knew a person didn't recover. They moved on. Went back to living. But they were never the same.

The sloppy direction of his thoughts had him drifting, his gaze on Marlowe and the long, sleek ponytail taming what he knew to be lush, deep brown hair that fell just below her shoulders. A rich shade of brown that matched the deep, coffee-colored hue of her eyes.

Which also meant his mind was quite a ways away

when the shouts and clapping around the table pulled him back.

Marlowe's smile was triumphant as she stepped away from the conference table, the safe now open. She'd already turned her back on it, clearly uninterested in what was inside, but the forensics team had beat her to the loot anyway.

And pulled two kilo-sized bags of heroin out of the gaping mouth of the safe.

Chapter 2

"We ID'd your East River vic," Detective Arlo Prescott said, tossing a folder on Wyatt's desk.

Wyatt looked up, Arlo's smug smile only palatable because he'd brought the news Wyatt was looking for and he was a damn fine detective.

It helped that they'd also been friends since the seventh grade, their mutual love of comic books and eighth grade dream girl Emma Wilson bonding them young.

Arlo had the added bragging rights that came from snagging a dance with Emma at their middle school spring fling, before being left heartbroken when she'd confessed her family was moving to New Jersey at the end of the school year. While Jersey was less than twenty miles away, Bergen County might as well have been San Francisco for two young men of thirteen.

And while Emma Wilson had departed their lives for some unimagined future in the Garden State, Wyatt and Arlo had managed to keep their friendship intact for twenty years.

"If you're here to tell me his name is Luke Decker, age thirty-nine, resident of a slightly questionable building in the Lower East Side, I already know."

"Son of a bitch," Arlo muttered before dropping into the guest chair beside Wyatt's desk. "How'd you get the details?"

"I dragged him off the floor of the East River. It comes with a few privileges."

Arlo slammed a hand on the desk, the old metal still echoing when he lifted the same hand to run it through crow-black hair. "I knew Stacy Brunell in forensics liked you better."

"Everyone likes me better than you." Wyatt couldn't help grinning at his friend. "It's a trial, to be sure, but I'm up to the task."

"Last I checked, everyone, that is, but Marlowe McCoy."

Wyatt caught himself before allowing that fact—one that was 100 percent true—to settle his face in dark lines. Marlowe McCoy seemed to go out of her way to ignore him and it regularly stuck in his craw like a fist.

Unaware or willing to ignore the results of his jab, Arlo pressed on. "Heard she was the one who opened the safe the other day."

"Yep. Smooth as silk, as usual. She had it open in under ninety seconds."

Arlo let out a low whistle. "That's impressive, even

for her. I heard it took Middleton nearly a half hour to manage the first one."

Jasper Middleton was Marlowe's chief competitor in Sunset Bay and throughout most of Brooklyn, really. And while he got his fair share of jobs—and considerably smaller payments—the 86th had finally gotten smart and started calling Marlowe in when they knew they could get the budget for her services. She didn't come cheap, but she was quicker and she'd yet to contaminate evidence. A feat Jasper didn't share.

"That's why he wasn't called in on the second or third."

Arlo shook his head. "Three, Trumball. What the hell's going on?"

It was the same question that had haunted Wyatt for two days and he hadn't come up with anything that made sense. Three safes, all strapped to bodies that drowned in the waters around New York. Three victims with kill shots to the chest. Same cause of death and same strange manner of discovery, but not a single connection any of them could find between three dead men in less than a month.

Canvasses of the victims' respective neighborhoods—Murray Hill for the first, Hell's Kitchen for the second—hadn't produced anything viable. And with the news of the third victim's residence far away from the first two, Wyatt wasn't holding out much hope they'd find any connections now, either.

With that foremost in his thoughts, Wyatt opened the folder to see what the coroner had come up with. Although he'd enjoyed teasing Arlo, beyond the name of the victim and basic details, he'd been waiting on the full report for the past two days.

And as he scanned the report he saw the same details that had littered the files of first victim, Sammy Robards, and second victim, Jayden Phillips. Men nearing middle age who were moving through the waters around New York in kayaks, safes seemingly strapped to their chests by choice, and a lone kill shot to the chest, just above the top of the safe.

None had anything show up on their toxicology reports, nor were any of them tattooed with any particular markings. Which made three men who'd all died the same way with nothing in common except the way they'd died.

"You think we've got a serial killer?"

"We have serial behavior but these guys are making this choice." Wyatt tapped the folder. "No sign of a struggle on the bodies or underneath the bungee cords wrapping the safe to their bodies. All were seemingly enjoying a day out on the water when their kayaks turned under and bystanders called in the disappearance. And not a single bystander noticed the gunshots, which suggests silencer."

"Professionals, then."

"But professional what?" Wyatt flipped through the slim folder once more. "Even the heroin take in the safes is small potatoes. We'll take what we can get off the streets, of course, but it feels like a plant, you know?"

"You think someone's setting these guys up?"

"I don't know." Wyatt scrubbed a hand over his face before eyeing his friend. "All I do know is a lot of people are getting killed for the equivalent of a weekend worth of sales. I can't help but think we're sitting on the tip of the iceberg."

"Maybe you're right. But what are we missing?" Arlo reached for the folder and flipped through it, his attention focused and his gaze sharp as always.

If only they could find the connection, Wyatt thought. That's what they needed to move this along. And up until now, except for the cause and manner of death, they had nothing.

Nothing, of course, but three dead guys.

Marlowe unwrapped the various items in the steaming bag of takeout and questioned the wisdom of filling her eighty-two-year-old grandfather with fried rice and panfried pot stickers. And then, as she caught the scent of all that luscious pork emanating from the dumplings and the enticing scents of shrimp from the rice, she decided she needed to live a little.

And stilled herself mid-wince when she heard Pops uncap the tops of two beers—light, at least—from the fridge.

This was their standing dinner each week and takeout night was sacrosanct. Even if she was perpetually concerned about his HDLs and his blood pressure.

"You live until you die, sweetie pie," had been Anderson McCoy's life philosophy for as long as Marlowe could remember. It was strangely of-the-moment yet equally unnerving when watching him stare at a plate of Chinese takeout with a mixture of avarice and happiness.

"You order from Dim Sum Emperor this time?" Her grandfather set their beers down on the small table in the corner of his kitchen before taking one of the seats with the cushion covers her grandmother had hand-embroidered.

"Yes."

"They have the best shrimp fried rice in Brooklyn."

"You always say that but Dumpling Palace is my favorite."

"Amateurs." Her grandfather blew a raspberry her way as he placed his napkin in his lap. "Dim Sum Emperor has oil in their woks that's older than Dumpling Palace."

"And we're calling that a good thing?"

He laughed as he reached for his beer. "I'm just teasing you. You know I'm not picky as long as I get dinner with my girl."

"I still think we could try a salad from time to time. They put a great place in over on Water Street. You pick all the fixins' you want, along with a protein, and then top it with one of like thirty dressings."

"I eat healthy enough the rest of the week. I'm indulging when I'm with you. Besides, we have something a lot more interesting to talk about tonight than takeout. I heard you caught another safe this week."

She couldn't hold back the smile at his interest, the excitement in his eyes far more pronounced for details on the case than they'd been for the rice.

"How'd you hear about that?"

"I know the 86th and the 86th knows me." He said the words with no small measure of pride and, again, Marlowe couldn't hold back her smile.

Her grandfather did know the 86th and he kept up

a strong pulse on the happenings inside the precinct. Where his granddaughter was involved, that went double.

"They made the mistake of calling Middleton in on the first safe."

Anderson shook his head. "I taught them better."

Marlowe shrugged as she reached for her beer. "Everyone's always watching their budgets until they get crappy results."

"'Buy cheap, buy often,' your grandmother always said."

That had been one of her grandmother's favorite sayings, even if it had always made Marlowe strangely sad. While she understood the adage for what it was, it made her think of her father. His tastes had never run toward the cheap version of anything and he was now sitting inside a maximum security facility upstate because of it.

Though, she had to admit somewhat philosophically, her father preferred his luxury items for free, lifted by his own hands, so perhaps cheap or expensive wasn't the right description for her father's tastes.

"Lowe—" Her grandfather's question hovered beneath his nickname for her. "You with me?"

"Yes. Of course." She pushed a bit of brightness into her smile. "Just working on not taking the Middleton selection too personally."

She'd never gotten much past him. His naturally keen perception and the dedication of his life's work to solving crimes making him pretty much unbeatable when it came to telling him lies of any sort, even the small white ones.

Which made the fact he overlooked her small slip both a surprise and a relief.

"Everyone has a budget they can't stretch when they're dealing with the first crime. By the time they get a repeat the purse strings loosen a bit. Three safes in four weeks has everyone asking questions."

"And those purse strings are considerably looser." Marlowe thought of the invoice she sent in that very afternoon.

"Exactly. And I have no doubt my very talented granddaughter is worth every penny."

"You sure you're not biased?"

He shot her a wink as he reached for his beer. "I can be biased and right."

Since he was both, she took it in stride and settled in to hear her grandfather's theories. As the chief of detectives for the 86th for more than twenty-five years, he loved a good mystery and took great pride in the number of cases his team closed while he was in charge.

"You see what was in the safe? I know you don't always look."

"I look, I just don't care what's inside."

"You really don't?"

It wasn't the first time they'd had this conversation, but despite her grandfather's unwavering support of her, he refused to believe she wasn't interested in the safes she opened for the cops.

Or for anyone else for that matter.

Whether it was a deliberate mental block to diligently avoid her father's life choices or the bigger fact that she just didn't care what people hoarded or hid, cracking a safe for the thrill of beating it had always interested her far more than what it held inside.

It had also felt good to create a business from scratch.

Something that was uniquely her own, and physical proof that she wasn't her father. That she didn't thrive on taking things from other people.

"Heard Wyatt Trumball's working the case."

Marlowe felt that distinct stiffening in her shoulders whenever Wyatt's name came up and tried to keep her tone casual. Even if her back had already gone poker-straight. "As much as the Harbor team does. I heard he's sharing the actual detective work with the team."

Although she tried hard not to focus too much on Wyatt Trumball or the damnable fascination with him that never seemed to fully go away, she was admittedly curious about his work. While he was a full member of the NYPD, his specialized skills in scuba kept him in the water more than working cases on land. As she understood it, once he'd made detective, he'd shared the load with someone firmly land-based to work the crime.

"A mystery wrapped up in a crime?" Pops asked. "Everyone wants a piece of something like that."

Since it was clear her long-retired grandfather wanted a piece of it, too, she couldn't help but key in on his words. "You think something's going on?"

"Crimes like that? They feel like a plant or a taunt." Pops set down his fork. "I never trusted crimes that felt incomplete."

"What does that mean? Incomplete?"

"Criminals running drugs or numbers or gangs, they have a rhythm. A ritual. These unconnected kayakers with small caches of heroin? It's off, you know."

She did know. Even if she didn't care about what was actually inside the safes she opened, Marlowe knew enough of her grandfather's and her father's work to know that exact rhythm he spoke of. For all that was illegal, those successful in criminal enterprises often were because they worked at it, just like any other business. It was sad those individuals didn't know how to channel their abilities toward better outcomes, but human nature never was, nor would it ever be, fully understandable.

But it was predictable.

She nearly said as much when the doorbell to her grandfather's ground-floor apartment rang. "You expecting company?"

"I invited Detective Trumball over."

"You invited Wyatt?"

Her grandfather's gaze got suspiciously busy on the small edge of his beer label as he tugged at a frayed corner. "Told him I'd like to hear about the case. Get his thoughts. Shoot a few ideas around with him."

Pops set the beer down and stood to head for the door, but she laid a hand on his arm before he could get moving.

"I'll get it." She glanced at their nearly finished dinners. "But you could have let me know to get more food."

"He didn't want to interrupt our dinner, but he did promise he'd pick up pie from Lucille's." Those distinct hints of avarice were back in her grandfather's gaze. "Boston crème."

Marlowe avoided groaning, even as she mentally tallied the impacts of fried rice and rich, sugary cream on her grandfather's digestive system. And then she stopped for a moment and really looked at him.

Although age and the trials of life had taken their

toll, carving lines in his face and threading white nearly over his entire head, Anderson McCoy still cut an impressive figure. Six foot two, with shoulders that had slimmed with age but still weren't stooped, he knew who he was and he knew how to take care of himself.

And he'd invited Wyatt Trumball over for dessert.

She didn't think her grandfather knew her frustrating, yet always electric feelings for the man, but she wouldn't put anything past him.

But now it was time to answer the bell.

And avoid thinking about how she was going to get through the next hour without showing a single hint of the attraction she felt for the man standing outside her grandfather's front door.

Wyatt stared down at the pastry box with the swirling, swooping neon pink letters that spelled out Lucille's and tried to tamp down on the anticipation that had grown steadily stronger as he wove his way through Sunset Bay toward the old brownstone on Chestnut Street.

He'd spent months trying to persuade Marlowe McCoy to go out with him on a date, all to no avail. Yet now here he was, ready to have dessert with her and her grandfather. A man who was both a legend at the 86th precinct and also as sharp at eighty-two as he had no doubt been at twenty-two.

Which meant Wyatt had better put his game face on because he couldn't let the former chief of detectives at the 86th see just how enamored he was of the man's granddaughter.

"Wyatt. Hello." Marlowe stood in the open doorway,

the front door of Anderson's apartment just off the inside hallway of the brownstone. "And you brought pie."

"I brought Lucille's pie," he said, emphasizing the woman's name, legendary throughout the borough. "With her compliments to your grandfather, by the way."

Marlowe smiled at that, the first genuine smile he could recall seeing from her. "Those two flirt terribly every time he's in her shop."

"I thought your grandfather was a man of action. Lucille's single, as far as I know. Why are they just flirting?"

She shot him a side eye while gesturing him through the door. "Aren't you a bit too young to play matchmaker?"

"Is it matchmaking if they're already interested in each other?"

"A good matchmaker knows where to gently push," she whispered low as they crossed the living room that sat adjacent to the kitchen, "and when to walk away."

Since it sounded suspiciously like the lyrics of a country and western song—or a distinct warning to back off—Wyatt opted to take full advantage of the need to clarify her statement.

Both because he was wired that way and because hell, it was just fun.

With a few remaining seconds to get in the last word, he leaned close. "What fun is it to back off?"

"I'd say, where's the fun in being a persistent pest?"

"Just like the matchmaking, it's only being a pest if it's unwelcome."

It was a long shot, but even no more than ten feet

from his precinct's most respected retired officer, Wyatt wanted to see if he could make a dent in Marlowe's very attractive—and totally locked down—visage. Especially since it was obvious they were no longer talking about Anderson and Lucille.

He took the rising heat in her pretty brown eyes as a point for him.

Before she could respond, he turned his attention to the 86th's living legend. He still felt Marlowe's heated gaze on him as he set the box on the small kitchen table in front of Anderson, adding, "With Lucille's compliments."

"That woman works wonders."

"That she does. And I hear she puts a little extra love in her Boston crème."

If Anderson was aware of Wyatt's deliberate taunts, he kept his poker face on, instead standing and crossing the small space to the cabinets, pulling down plates. "Lowe, let's put some coffee on."

"You don't want another beer?"

Anderson's brows rose. "With pie?"

She shrugged before turning her attention to Wyatt. "Beer or coffee?"

"Definitely coffee. Thank you." He used the small space of the kitchen to stand a bit closer than actually needed. "If you let me know where the knives are, I can cut the pie."

He delighted in the slight rise of color on her cheeks and more of that confused heat in her dark eyes before she pointed toward a nearby drawer. "In there."

Was it possible she wasn't completely unaffected?

Sure, he was being deliberate but the kitchen was

also small. He and Anderson had already moved around
one another dealing with the pie box.

Wyatt's thoughts from a few days before in the precinct conference room came back to him. He wasn't a
man who pursued women who weren't interested. It was
a useless exercise that diminished the mutual fun of a
happy, healthy relationship. But there'd always been
something about Marlowe McCoy that, in spite of the
distinct freeze he always got in her presence, made it
hard to walk away.

Was there a hint of something in their interactions
that his gut recognized better than his head?

It was a tempting thought but his repeated attempts
to take her to breakfast after their morning runs had
suggested otherwise.

Resolving to think about it later, he found the knife
in the exact place Marlowe had indicated and returned
to the table where Anderson already had the decadent
dessert pulled from the box. In a matter of minutes,
they had a round of coffee, steaming from mismatched,
chipped mugs, and plates with very generous helpings
of Lucille's love-filled Boston crème.

He'd expected a drubbing from Marlowe for the
slices he'd cut but she'd dug into her giant piece with
gusto.

A far cry from what he was used to.

Just like the mugs and the small kitchen, he mused as
he discreetly looked around. Although he hadn't been
born with a silver spoon, his mother had found her way
easily enough into the high life when their family circumstances changed. The estate she now lived in on
Long Island had never felt like home, and not just be-

cause they'd moved there his junior year of high school, with few of his formative years left in the place.

"You've caught quite a case." Anderson's excitement was evident as he scooped up a forkful of pie. "People have been subtle in what they're saying, but it's not hard to read between the lines."

Grateful for the distraction, Wyatt set his fork down, his smile easy. "And you made it your life's work to read between those lines."

Anderson shrugged, the move surprisingly hale for a man of his age. "It's the job. And, strange but true, it's life."

The NYPD had mandatory retirement at age sixty-three. The fact that Anderson had been out of the game for nearly two decades was at odds with the clear skill and enjoyment he had for police work.

"Would you please tell him I didn't nose around the insides of the safe, either?" Marlowe let out a small huff. "Even knowing me my entire life, he refuses to believe me."

"Maybe because it's impossible to understand how a highly competent, accomplished woman like yourself isn't the tiniest bit curious about the safes you open."

"They're none of my business."

"But they hold mysteries," Wyatt argued, still unable to comprehend how she could be so casual about it all. "And come on, you have to have seen some doozies in your line of work. I know you do more than police work. Tell us, what are some of the most interesting things you've opened?"

"I don't discuss the confidential aspects of my work. And the problem is you two, anyway."

"Us?" Her grandfather looked surprised.

"You two live in a world where you're convinced there are things hidden between those lines you're both so fond of. I live in a far simpler place. Things are locked. I unlock them. It's binary."

She spoke of her job with a simplicity and while he didn't fully agree, Wyatt had to admit that he understood it on some level. Diving was a binary profession, too. You were above the water or under it. Your equipment worked or it didn't. You found something or you came up empty-handed.

The only difference, he supposed, was that each time he came up with something, it had ripple effects far beyond the water.

Like mysterious safes strapped to dead men.

Or the ever-present memories of his father, who'd died beneath the water, too.

Chapter 3

If she hadn't been looking at him, Marlowe would have missed the flash of sadness in Wyatt's gaze.

And if she were fair, sadness wasn't even a remotely accurate description. There was a deep sorrow that she'd never seen in his expression before.

But you've felt it.

The idea haunted her, even as she rolled it over in her mind. For all Wyatt's teasing and good-natured taunts, she did recognize those hidden depths in him. And if she were even more honest, she'd detected it from the start. It was part of what drew her to him, even as she rejected the idea of having anyone look too closely at the sad parts inside her that she deliberately hid from the world.

Suddenly needing something to do, Marlowe collected their plates and put them in the sink. She turned to reach for the coffeepot, intending to bring it back to the table, and ran into Wyatt's very solid chest.

He held up the pot, out of reach of spilling hot coffee onto them. "Do you want a refill?"

"Sure. That'd be great."

His gaze captured hers and held for the briefest moment, those deep blue depths calming her racing thoughts. And then he winked, the move just ridiculous enough that it had her backing away and marching back to her seat.

Damn, the man knew how to get to her.

Which meant it was time to get them firmly back on track.

"Putting aside your disdain for my thoughts on the contents of cracked safes," she asked as she took her seat, "what do you both really think is going on with these kayakers strapped to safes?"

"I wish I knew." Wyatt finished topping off everyone's mugs. "The whole thing smacks of a setup of some sort, but there's no connection between the victims."

Captivated, her grandfather stilled, his mug halfway to his lips. "Not a thing?"

"Nothing. They're from different neighborhoods with no apparent connections with their families, schools or jobs. We've found no discernable matches on their social media pages and nothing to suggest they even used the same types of kayaks or sporting equipment."

"Strangers to each other," Marlowe murmured.

"That's a clue, though." Her grandfather had remained quiet as Wyatt spoke of various aspects of the case, but it was clear that he was not only paying close attention but processing each detail carefully.

"How so, Pops?"

"Consider the fact that nothing connects these individuals yet they've died in the exact same way. Their killer connects them which means there's some method to how the killer found them. Or used them," Anderson added, almost as an afterthought.

"Used them?" Wyatt's always-sharp gaze went as cold and as lethal as an ice pick.

"What if the killer handpicked them for some purpose?"

"Which means the killer's the thread." Marlowe marveled at the simplicity of the idea. And how quickly her grandfather had taken the lack of connection and seen such a clear link between them all.

"You're a legend for a reason."

"No." Anderson smiled, clearly pleased by Wyatt's compliment. "I'm just an old dog who has seen all the tricks."

"Maybe, but it's a big idea and something for us to dig into. Thank you."

"Thanks for making this old dog feel a bit younger for an hour."

Marlowe reached across the table and laid a hand over her grandfather's. "I keep telling you, you're vintage."

"And Lucille seems awfully fond of you," Wyatt added, his voice considerably lighter than when discussing dead bodies pulled from the water.

Marlowe shot Wyatt a look, irritated at his insistence on pushing a possible romance between her grandfather and Brooklyn's most accomplished sugar pusher when something pulled her up short.

Along with that sorrow she'd detected earlier, now she saw something else in his smile.

A genuineness that suggested Wyatt Trumball might not be the good-natured cop with a quick quip she'd thought him to be. For the past few years, each time she'd been in his company she'd written him off as a cocky cop who took nothing seriously.

But tonight had suggested something else.

A man with a sharp eye and deeper feelings than she'd ever given him credit for.

It was humbling.

And, against her better judgment, deeply appealing.

Although he was enjoying himself, Wyatt knew it was time to get going. He'd gotten what he'd come for—help from a cop who'd likely forgotten more than Wyatt would ever know—and the added benefit of some time with the man's granddaughter.

But he needed to give them their evening back.

So it was a surprise when Anderson started barking orders.

"You drive over here, Detective?"

"Yes, I did." Although he had no interest in living the same lifestyle as his mother, Wyatt had willingly taken on the expense of keeping his own SUV in the city. The expense of a car—and the needed monthly investment in a parking garage—was a bill he happily paid each month for the convenience of having his own transportation.

"Then you can drive Marlowe home."

She'd been busy collecting her things from a small chair in the living room—the large leather bag he knew she carried her tools in and what looked to be a small bag of fruit she'd purchased en route to her grandfather's—and immediately started to protest.

"I'm calling a car, Pops. Wyatt doesn't need to drive me."

"Of course I will."

"But I'm out of your way," she offered up lamely, even as resignation already lined her gaze.

"Park Slope's not that big. I'll drive you."

"You live in the same neighborhood?" Anderson asked Wyatt, seemingly delighted.

The overbright smile he added assured Wyatt the older man was well aware of where he lived.

"Not around the corner from me," Marlowe huffed.

"Come on." Wyatt reached for her bag, not surprised at the heft needed to carry the tools of her trade. "I got lucky and got a spot just out front."

She looked ready to argue—on the ride or his possession of her tools, he didn't know which—when she turned on her heel and hugged her grandfather. "I'll call you tomorrow."

"Not if I call you first."

The tight hug between the two lodged hard in Wyatt's chest and he turned slightly to give them privacy, surprised by how that familial ease sent a quick shot of envy zinging through his veins.

And then she was brushing past him, reaching for the door. It was only when she stopped and called her goodbyes over her shoulder that Wyatt was able to move in and open the front door of the apartment for her.

"See you next week, Pops."

"Have fun."

The slightest suggestion of a head shake ruffled the ends of her hair, but that was the only other indication Wyatt got that Marlowe was going to give her grandfather a talking-to at her next opportunity.

Instead, he was treated to her back as she marched toward the front door of the brownstone, dragging the heavy wood open on one hard swing.

Whatever advantage he'd earned through the evening was at risk of evaporating if he didn't retrench. So he moved quickly down the front stoop, clicking the alarm and locks off on his SUV, narrowly beating her long-legged stride to the passenger side door.

"Please. Let me." He had the door open before shifting to the back door. "I'll just set your tools back here."

Wyatt was careful as he set the bag down, aware she carried several fine-tuned instruments as well as heavier objects like drills.

"Thanks." He heard the comment from where she buckled in, heartened by the softening in her tone.

And then he was around the car and pulling out of the parking space, a sedan with its blinker on already waiting behind them to pull right in.

"Your grandfather's quite a man. I wasn't kidding when I called him a legend."

As conversational openers went, Wyatt figured it was safe territory and it helped that he meant every word. Anderson McCoy had given him a lot to think about tonight and his laser focus on the killer was a huge step forward. He, Arlo and the rest of the team had briefly discussed the killer but all of them had continued focusing on the victims.

It was good work and had still given them the details

that there wasn't a connection between the three men, but now it was time to shift their focus.

"Thank you for spending so much time with him. He was happier tonight than I've seen him in weeks." She turned to face him, the red glow of the stoplight in front of them hazing her features. "Not that he's not a happy person."

Wyatt took in that ready defense, curious she even felt the need to qualify the comment. "Once a cop, always a cop. It gets in your blood."

"If given the opportunity, I don't think he ever would have retired."

"An admirable state, but we're forced to retire for a reason. The job's a lot. And the risks are real, too."

"Which is why I'm very glad there is mandatory retirement."

She let out a light laugh, the husky overtones tightening his body. With it, he flexed his grip on the steering wheel, willing himself to ignore the attraction.

She's not interested, Trumball, no matter how much you might wish otherwise.

He took the last turn onto Fourth Avenue and in moments they were driving through Park Slope. He'd lived in Brooklyn nearly his entire life, those last two years in his mother's home when he was in high school the exception, but he considered this particular neighborhood in the borough his home.

"I love it here."

"The neighborhood?" He saw the hint of a smile at her lips before he returned his attention to navigating the considerably lighter evening traffic. "I do, too. My shop's just down there." She pointed toward a cross street, even though he already knew where she kept her business.

"While I do know that, I don't know your address. Want to direct me the rest of the way?"

"Sure." She instructed him to turn a few more lights down before surprising him with her next comment. "Packets of hair."

"What?"

"You asked me earlier what was the weirdest thing I'd ever seen in a safe. It was packets of hair." She let out an audible shiver at the memory. "I was afraid the guy was a serial killer but it turns out it was his own hair. He was an eccentric millionaire who'd saved every lock of hair from every haircut he'd had since the day he made his first million."

"Wow, you really can't underestimate how strange people can be."

"No, you can't."

"Is that why you don't like looking in safes?"

"Again, it's more that I don't care. Whatever people keep, no matter how weird or creepy or even just mundane, really isn't any of my business."

"But for that period of time, while the safe is in your possession, it very much is your business."

"I've spent too much of my life judging others for being voyeurs over my life. I have no desire to be the same."

The words were nearly out of his mouth to ask why when a biker shot out in front of him. Wyatt slammed on the brakes, his hand immediately reaching for her arm to hold her back. Her skin was soft beneath his fingertips and he let go as quickly as he'd reached out, feeling like he'd been singed.

The action was fairly pointless—the seat belts did their job and he hadn't been going that fast to begin with—but the move had been sheer instinct.

Even as the light, electrifying impression of touching her still coursed over his fingers.

"Sorry about that."

"The joys of city driving."

With his body quickly taking over his thoughts, he'd already drifted away from their conversation before the biker, so it was a surprise when she began speaking, her tone nervous and faster than he'd heard her before.

"Do you have any leads on the guy killing the kayakers?" She added a small, nervous laugh. "Or to be fair, I guess it could be a woman, too."

"We've got nothing. But with your grandfather's inputs tonight I'm definitely getting the team to shift focus ASAP."

"Do you do detective work and dive?"

"Yes and no. Because my diving is such a specialized skill, I'm paired with landlubbers for the work."

"Landlubbers?" She let out another laugh but this one wasn't deep and throaty. Instead it held more of those nervous overtones that suggested something had changed.

The ready conversation when she'd been fairly reluctant to give him the time of day up to now had his antennae quivering. And with it, he cycled back over their conversation.

I've spent too much of my life judging others for being voyeurs over my life. I have no desire to be the same.

And there it was.

How had he forgotten something so momentous about her?

He suspected her nervous and rapid shift in subject was a tactic to make him forget the comment entirely. It was likely the same reason she'd so quickly defended her grandfather's happiness, too.

Anderson and Marlowe might make a team, grandfather and granddaughter in lockstep with one another, but a generation used to exist between them. Anderson's son had been convicted in spectacular fashion, of grand larceny. A master thief, the headlines had read, operating throughout the city. Decades of Michael McCoy's crimes had come to light after he was caught about thirteen years before. His convictions a year later had been legendary and had earned him a lifetime stay at a maximum security prison upstate.

Anderson had already been retired and Wyatt hadn't been on the force all that long, but the story of Michael McCoy's conviction had been big news. Rumors had flown that the discovery of his son's crimes had nearly ruined Anderson, the betrayal cutting him in two.

For whatever reason, while it was a fact Wyatt knew, he'd never fully connected it to Marlowe as a problem that continued to linger in her life. He'd been attracted, yes, and deeply interested in her.

So how had he totally overlooked this aspect of her life?

He knew what it was to find your adult life formed by your parents.

How much harder would that be when it came through such a deep betrayal?

* * *

Stupid, stupid, stupid.

The thought had run through her mind over and over as she tried desperately to regroup.

Had Wyatt caught her slip?

She'd only brought up the dumb story about the hair in the safe to get them onto a harmless, silly topic. A dumb story that was just weird enough to draw interest.

And then she'd slipped about her father.

Or, if not exactly about him, about her reaction to him.

She directed Wyatt to the last few turns on her street. "I'm there, about three quarters of the way down the block."

He nodded just as someone's taillights flicked on. With the smooth ease of a born-and-bred New Yorker, Wyatt pulled to the side and put on his own blinker, waiting for the parking spot that would open shortly.

"You can just drop me off."

"And miss landing this prime spot?" He flashed her a grin and she tried—honestly, she really tried—to ignore how a riot of butterflies launched in her stomach at that smile.

Goodness, the man was lethal. And the solid length of his forearm that she'd admired on the entire drive, from where he had his hand propped on the steering wheel to where he reached down to the gear shift to put the SUV into Reverse to allow the car leaving a bit more room, had been distracting in the extreme.

Was that the reason for her slip? Because it was nearly impossible to keep her full wits and corresponding armor in place when her body insisted on noticing every damn thing about the man next to her.

Those forearms.

That grin.

Even the way his broad shoulders filled the button-down shirt he'd worn for the evening. A shirt, she suddenly realized, that was at odds with his normal uniform of T-shirt and jeans.

Had he dressed up to come over to have dessert with her and Pops?

Dress to impress, baby girl.

Her father's words lit up her mind, a steady reminder of his always-present focus on running some sleight of hand. From dressing to get people to see him in a certain way to building confidence with a mark to running an extensive and elaborate heist, Michael McCoy did nothing without purpose.

Add on his purpose was rarely good or altruistic and she had her father's personality in a nutshell.

One that had been filling her mind far too often these past few weeks. Was it his impending parole hearing, set for early October?

Or just the increasing realization that his hearing was coming after more than a decade in prison? A twelve-year stretch that had seen her grandmother die, her own business build and grow and her own father—one who was alive and well—missing out on every single year of her twenties.

Wyatt expertly maneuvered into the space, his parallel parking skills truly exceptional. And then he was jumping out of the SUV and walking around to let her out, a move that she would have seen coming if she didn't have her head so far up her ass with the memories that had been extra difficult of late.

Since it would have been poor form to step out when he was nearly around the car, she waited until he had the passenger side open. The spot he'd snagged was just over a drainage grate and he extended a hand to her. "Careful. It's a bit of a drop if you don't hit the sidewalk."

His grip was firm, solid, and she felt the unmistakable zing of heat trip up her arm as he helped her out. He then dropped her hand and headed for the back door to retrieve her tools.

"You don't have to carry those."

"Consider this the door-to-door treatment." His smile was wide, knowing and delectably cocky once more. "And something you won't get from a ride service."

She should be irritated. Really, she should. But how long had it been since she'd just walked somewhere with a man who was being gentlemanly and considerate? It was only a half a block walk, so it wouldn't do to make a mental fuss about it, but it was nice.

And since her bag ran about twenty-five pounds, it was extra nice not to be the one lugging her stuff for a change.

"Thanks for carrying my bag of rocks."

"That's what's in here?" He turned toward her as they walked down the sidewalk. "I was wondering."

"It's not all stethoscopes and grease pencils to open a safe."

"They still make those?"

She caught his grin a moment before she was ready

to respond seriously to the question. "The grease pencils? They do if you shop at the right art stores."

"Well, then, that's why I didn't realize they still exist. I avoid shopping whenever possible."

The laughter came smooth and easy and it was a surprise to realize she felt comfortable with him. In fact, if she were honest, she'd felt comfortable all evening. On high alert because of the attraction, but those nerves had been mixed with an underlying easy feeling when with someone you innately recognized.

Chemistry, her mother had called it when she was a kid.

A state Patty McCoy spoke of dreamily before shifting gears and lamenting how it had gotten her into trouble with Marlowe's father, which inevitably turned the discussion in a sour direction.

And which ultimately stopped happening at all when her mother filed for divorce and headed off to "find herself" somewhere in the deserts of Arizona. A place, last Marlowe knew, Patty still called home.

Just like earlier with her father, those memories of her parents were way too close to the surface. They kept tripping her up and made her feel as if the past decade hadn't even happened. Like she was a perpetual teenager, struggling to understand where she fit in a world of two selfish people who had a child they had never quite known what to do with.

"So how about if I meet you here tomorrow morning? Around six? We can take a run through the park and then I'll buy you breakfast."

"I'd like that."

She would?

Wait.

What?

Marlowe struggled to reorient herself to the conversation, from thoughts of chemistry with Wyatt to all the supposed trouble it had gotten her mother into.

And then she looked up at him—really looked at him—as they came to a stop at her front stoop and realized that while she should cancel their plans, she didn't want to.

Was that the problem with chemistry? It confused the mind until bad decisions were suddenly the only ones that made sense.

Before she could consider those implications for too long, he bent his head, pressing his lips to hers. Warm, soft and surprisingly chaste, Marlowe had just closed her eyes when Wyatt lifted his head.

"I'll see you tomorrow then."

"I—" She stammered before catching herself. Like with his help out of the car, arguing would only make her look petty and small and she hated being either. "Six. Sure."

He lifted her leather bag of tools, extending his hand with her precious cargo. She knew just how heavy that bag was and imagined the way his biceps flexed underneath the long sleeve of his dress shirt. Could see how those enticing muscles of his forearm tightened with the weight. And then she took the bag, noticing the warmth of his body had transferred to the leather handle.

"Thanks for bringing me home."

"You're welcome."

She stood there another moment, half convinced he'd say something brash and arrogant to mess things up. Only he kept his gaze steady and his mouth decidedly shut.

Which only served to confuse her more.

Ducking her head, she headed up the stairs. Her sole focus became getting the front door of her brownstone open and inside to her converted second-floor apartment before she made a bigger fool of herself.

It was only when she closed the front door firmly behind herself, waiting to hear the lock catch, that she looked through the wide pane of glass that made up most of the facing on the door.

Wyatt still stood at the bottom of the stoop, a thoughtful expression on his face.

And there wasn't a cocky grin in sight.

Chapter 4

Once again, she cursed herself for the ready agreement to the early morning run and breakfast, but as she laced up her sneakers, Marlowe also recognized there was no way out of it.

Wyatt Trumball was so smooth, so casual, so...

So interesting.

And hell, she admitted as she snagged her phone off the dresser and stared herself dead in the eye in the mirror. "You want to go."

Because the truth was, for all her frustration in his presence, she wasn't blind to his good qualities. The man was an outstanding cop and diver, impressive traits in their own right, but lethal as a combination. He was exceptionally well respected at the 86th and her grandfather was a fan, which was a testament to Wyatt's character. And his incredibly attractive body was a temple, but he wasn't pristine or annoying with it if last night's pie was any indication.

She'd believed for years the benefit of getting up and running every morning—aside from the opportunity to deal with the roiling, swirling thoughts that had found a way in since childhood—was so that she could eat the things she wanted guilt free.

Wyatt's sheer enjoyment last night over coffee and pie made her suspect he might feel the same.

And that was a special quality, too.

The ability to enjoy the moment. And to acknowledge—in that moment—that what you had was enough.

She'd begun to realize the importance of that philosophy a few years before. The twin understanding that Pops wouldn't be around forever and that her father had lived his own life never believing that he had enough was a realization that had gone down quite hard. But after that initial burst of anger and sadness, the bitter flavor of that reality began to shift her perspective.

It had been the shock to her system that forced her to recognize that the only person who could make her life what she wanted it to be was her.

The only life she had to live was hers.

So why had she always been so tetchy and reticent around Wyatt Trumball?

She dated. In fact, she'd had an enjoyable summer, finding herself out and about around the city most weekends. A Saturday spent walking the grounds of Governor's Island in early June with a college professor who lived in Red Hook had led to a few more dates before things sorted of drifted away. Not bad, per se, just… fizzled.

Then there was the cute gym instructor she'd met at a picnic in late July. They'd had a few fun weeks running around doing active things, but he'd had that whole "my body is a temple" vibe and she'd willingly let that one fade away on its own. Life was too short not to enjoy a doughnut on Sunday mornings, after all.

And then there was the incredibly promising date with the financier the Friday night of Labor Day weekend that she'd have happily extended her long weekend for, but he'd kissed her good night at her front door and proverbially disappeared.

Marlowe hadn't spent a lot of time worrying about any of them—or any of the men she'd dated that had come before—but now, as she headed for the park and her meet up with Wyatt, she had to wonder.

Why didn't anything ever stick?

Was there a streak of her father embedded way down when it came to relationships? Always something better out there, so don't get too close.

Don't get in too deep?

Or was it more the reality of growing up with a suave, slick and all-around feckless parent that had set the stage for her relationships?

All her relationships.

It was a convenient and handy excuse, but one she'd spent a lot of time working with a therapist on for that exact reason.

She didn't want excuses. Or handy reasons to explain the way she was.

She had to own who she was.

Just like knowing that living in the moment was all hers, Marlowe also had to own the choices she made.

Which brought her right back around to Wyatt.

For whatever reason, she'd made that choice today. And as she saw him in the distance, just where he'd said he'd be at the edge of the great lawn, something clutched tight in her chest before zinging out through the rest of her body like a wave.

The professor hadn't managed that. Nor had the sexy gym trainer. And while able to converse casually throughout a deeply enjoyable evening, Wall Street hadn't notched up her libido beyond a passing flash of interest.

So maybe she needed to cut herself a break. After all, attractive dinner companions were a dime a dozen.

Men who caused this sort of reaction?

Shockingly rare.

"Marlowe." Wyatt smiled up at her from where he bent, one leg extended on a park bench. "Come on and warm up."

She followed his lead, using the bench for support to go through the various stretches she'd use before and after her run. As she bent her forehead toward her knee, she kept her eyes on his, more of that heat flaring up and warming her far more effectively than any stretch could.

And as her gaze caught on his blue one, as bright as the cloudless sky above them, she had to admit one more thing.

Her summer dates had been fun and interesting and easy. No one who pushed her or tested her or made her think beyond breezy conversation and low-risk time together.

Wyatt Trumball would never fit that bill.

Was that why she'd denied him for so long? Because way down deep, on a level she hadn't even admitted to herself before, she recognized that?

As she deepened the stretch, Marlowe considered it all and had to admit it played. Like the last tumbler dropping into place, she could at least spend this morning in full acknowledgment of the truth.

Wyatt Trumball wasn't easy. Or simple. Or casual.

Perhaps it was time to lean into that instead of always dancing away.

Wyatt felt the change in the air as sure as the cool late summer breeze wafting around them hinted clearly of fall. Whatever disdain Marlowe usually brought to their encounters, he'd yet to find it this morning.

Had last night paid bigger dividends than he'd realized?

New lines to tug in his case and a more willing version of Marlowe McCoy?

Scratch willing, Wyatt thought, and amended himself to be more open. For the first time in all their interactions he could remember, he got the sense she wanted to be there and wanted to spend time with him. It had his pulse racing in a hard victory lap and he weighed impulse mere moments before deciding what the hell.

Leaning toward her, closing the small distance between their bodies, he pressed a kiss to her lips. It was chaste by any standard he could come up with, yet the mere touch of her lips against his had something racing through him faster than a lightning strike. The lone leg he still balanced on while the other was stretched against the bench trembled from the simple meeting of lips and he nearly toppled into her before catching himself and pulling his head back.

"Why'd you—" She took a deep breath before dropping her extended leg from the bench. "Why'd you do that?"

"Do you always ask a guy why he wanted to kiss you?"

"Most guys work up to it."

"I've been working up to it for a hell of a long time." The words came out practically as a growl and he pulled himself up out of his own stretch, both feet firmly back on the park path.

She looked ready to say something else before shifting gears. "Let's just get started."

He was tempted to talk more but he'd already pushed it with the kiss and, if he were honest, was already thinking about pushing his luck with another one.

Might as well shut your mouth, Trumball. Burn off a bit of this energy with exercise.

Which made her quick shout of "try and keep up!" a more-than-fair response to his unexpected kiss.

Marlowe was off like a shot, weaving her way straight down the park path and leaving quite a few other runners in her wake. He had just enough competitive spirit to take off after her, nonplussed by the "what the hell" and "watch out, man" he got as he added a second wave of cool breeze past the other joggers.

And he had to hand it to her five minutes later when they were still pacing side by side, yet basically racing each other through the running lane along Park Drive—there was something to be said for a woman who could challenge you.

Emotionally and physically.

His breath still came in even inhales and exhales, but her pace pushed him. Wyatt had never considered his morning runs lazy by any means, but this strenuous jog through the park had him working harder than usual. While he'd never taken his fitness for granted—and knew his ability to perform under the water was tightly aligned to his workouts—their run was a sign he needed to up his game in the morning.

They said little as they ran just shy of three and a half miles around the park, slowing as they closed in on the exact place they'd started on the inner loop. Sweat coated them as they retrieved the water bottles each of them had strapped to their hips, drinking deeply. Marlowe spoke first.

"I don't usually run with a partner. That was fun and it made me realize I've been slacking off lately. Just because I'm moving every morning doesn't mean I'm pushing myself."

"I thought the same. Especially when we hit mile marker two about five minutes before I usually do."

She laughed softly. "Thanks for pushing me."

"Right back at ya, Legs."

She eyed him over the water bottle where she'd lifted it to her lips for another swig. "We're back to that?"

"You do have extraordinary legs."

"So nice of you to notice."

Her tone was dry and he lowered his own bottle to look at her.

And in that moment, he was forced to admit the endless rounds of teasing—never ill-intentioned on his part—might not have been received in the same way.

"I've never meant it as an insult or an attempt to objectify you. But I am sorry if any of my teasing up to now has bothered you or hurt you. I'll do better."

"Thank you."

"Thank you for giving me a chance to apologize."

She seemed to consider something before coming to a decision. "You can make it up to me by buying me that breakfast you promised."

"Deal."

"Pancakes." She kept her gaze level. "With hash browns and bacon."

"You got it."

As they walked out of the park, side by side on their way to the Prospect Diner, he had to admit the truth.

It was far more enjoyable to spend time with her than trying to tease her to get a few seconds of her attention—simple wisps of her time—as scraps.

Far better, indeed.

Marlowe considered Wyatt's apology as she flipped through her menu. It was a mindless exercise since she already knew what she was ordering, but staring aimlessly at the menu gave her time to collect her thoughts.

Even as one thought whispered over and over in her mind.

Wyatt Trumball was an endless surprise.

I've never meant it as an insult or an attempt to objectify you.

I am sorry if any of my teasing up to now has bothered you or hurt you.

I'll do better.

Had anyone in her life ever apologized to her like that? With a response that was so swift, immediate and genuine?

Marlowe was damn sure that answer was a no.

I'll do better...

She set her menu down on the table and reached for the coffee their waitress had poured upon greeting them. Wyatt's menu was folded before him and his smile firmly in place, even as she saw the deeper thoughts swirling behind his blue eyes.

"You still getting the pancakes?"

"Absolutely." He patted his flat stomach. "What's the point of a workout if there's no reward after?"

"I will admit, that aspect is a surprise."

"What aspect?"

"You're an elite diver. I'll admit I expected a bit more of the 'my body is a temple' routine out of you." She took a sip of her coffee. "So I'm sorry for judging you."

"Thank you."

Although she was usually quite good at checking her impulses, something in her ironclad will to keep her thoughts to herself had seemingly vanished. "Why do we do that? As humans?"

"Do what?"

"Judge each other. Have expectations about each other? I don't know you, not really, yet I thought that about you."

"Aside from my deeply personal, lifelong love affair with pancakes and syrup, which you'd have no way of knowing, I wouldn't be too hard on yourself. You took a set of information you know to be true and you likely added in prior experiences with other people. It's a bit like detective work."

She was prevented from responding by the return of their waitress, but continued to chew on Wyatt's easygoing explanation as they put in their orders for a veritable breakfast feast.

After the woman was gone, Marlowe pressed on. "I think you're letting me off too easy."

He shrugged. "I don't. What's wrong with using prior experiences and the world around you to make assessments?"

"Even if those assessments are wrong?"

"You were willing to amend your beliefs when you got new information. That's part of detective work, too. You can't be so married to an outcome that you can't pivot when evidence comes to light and suggests a new direction."

It was an interesting thought and she had to admit he had a point. She had never wanted to be so intent in her opinions that she couldn't be persuaded when new information caused her to look at things in a new way or when an alternative dimension revealed itself.

Like admitting your father was a criminal?

Those memories had teeth and she fought them back, more used to them rearing their heads when she ran or when she lay in bed late at night, thinking over her family's sins.

Since those thoughts never failed to ruin her mood, she shifted gears. Opting to keep the conversation light—breezy even—she desperately willed those memories back to the places where they lurked.

"What do you do when you have no clues? Like those safes?"

"Then you work the angles until you find something."

As the memory receded it was replaced with the evening before and the excitement that had carried Pops through the discussion over pie.

"My grandfather really enjoyed talking to you last night about those angles. I could see it in his expression and the subtle excitement humming around him. Thank you for that."

"The thanks are all mine. His reputation is stellar and he has a lifetime of experience to draw on. I appreciate his time more than I can say."

Their waitress dropped off their breakfast plates and Marlowe and Wyatt busied themselves with doctoring their pancakes with butter and syrup. After the first few, delicious bites Wyatt picked up the thread.

"I was also interested by how quickly he connected the dead bodies. Or said another way, how their lack of a connection was a connection after all. And he just saw it, like it was no big deal."

"He was quick with that."

"It's like breathing to him," Wyatt said, a subtle sense of awe in his words. "I know it's experience, but even ten years in I can't imagine making connections so quickly and cleanly."

"Oh, I don't know. You've got quite a reputation, yourself, Detective Trumball."

"I've closed my fair share of cases but I'm not sure it's the same thing. That innate, instinctive knowing? It's something special."

"Do you come from a line of cops?"

"Nope, not a one. My father was a diver, too."

Although she'd not intended anything beyond making conversation, Marlowe recognized the subtle shift in tone. A casual carefulness that pushed beneath his words. One that was immediately visible in the way his eyes darkened, any sense of openness fading away.

"So you grew up in the water?"

"Something like that."

She'd spent her life avoiding conversation about her own father so Marlowe was adept at reading the signs from another person. The keen desire to keep her own family out of her conversations had her backing off.

"It's quite a unique skill."

"It's a living."

She wasn't quite sure that was true but gave him the conversational out. And despite their earlier apologies over their mutual misjudgments, Marlowe realized how easy it had been to talk to him, even then.

A state that was only clear now once it had vanished like smoke.

Instead, they shifted to the stilted small talk of people who didn't know each other that well. Summer blockbuster movies they'd both seen and a new show that dropped recently on one of the streaming services. Their inane conversation was absent of the same land mines they'd each stepped into that morning but, somehow, Marlowe couldn't find much interesting in their surface topics.

Which meant it wasn't exactly a surprise when Wyatt pulled money out of his wallet to lay on top of the check, abruptly standing to signal the end of their breakfast.

She followed him out the diner into the late summer sunshine, the heat already notched up about ten degrees since they walked in. "It's going to be hot today. Summer's not done with us yet."

"Should make for a pretty dive. My team's on bridge duty this week."

"Bridge duty?"

He walked beside her back down Prospect Park West, away from Grand Army Plaza and toward their mutual meeting place at the entrance to the park.

"It's not an aspect of the job we talk about broadly, but you have a fair amount of insider knowledge. The team regularly dives the bridges and tunnels to make sure nothing's been tampered with." He shrugged. "It's not classified, per se, but it's not widely advertised either."

"I'll keep it to myself."

He stopped and turned toward her. "I imagine you will."

I'll do better...

Marlowe wasn't entirely sure what she'd said earlier, but she recognized that she'd misstepped. It was only her odd, persistent desire to get that easier camaraderie back that had her slowing to a stop before speaking. "You were kind enough to apologize earlier and I feel I owe you one in return."

He turned toward her, his expression carefully blank. "For what?"

"I'm sorry if I overstepped about your family. I got the sense—" Marlowe broke off, Wyatt's gaze shielded by the sunglasses he'd slipped on when they'd walked out of the diner hiding whatever she believed she'd seen earlier. "I get the sense it was a bit of a third rail topic and I'm sorry."

He shrugged but he did drag the sunglasses off. That same darkness hadn't fully faded from his gaze, but she did get the slightest sense some weight had shifted off his shoulders. "You didn't overstep and I'm sorry if I clammed up. How about if we forget about it and put that one in the category of 'when I know you better'?"

"Right. Sure. Of course."

When she knew him better?

Considering the fact she'd been apprehensive of meeting him this morning it was a shock to realize her disappointment at his abrupt shut down.

Or the sudden fear that there wouldn't be another chance to get to know him better.

"Thanks for the workout this morning, Marlowe. I've been slacking on my fitness and it was good to push myself."

"You're welcome."

"I'd better get going."

"Of course. You've got a bridge to see to."

That surprise kiss he'd pressed on her before their run came back to mind and she was suddenly sorry she'd been so prickly about it earlier. Because an urge she couldn't dismiss kept up an insistent pressure in her mind.

If given the chance, she would like to kiss Wyatt again.

She'd like that very much.

Harry "Dutch" Kisco lifted the soldering iron from where he held it to the back edge of the safe, burning off the serial number. They'd been careful with the purchases of each safe, buying from different dealers and paying in cash, but it wouldn't do to have some enterprising cop backtrack the serial number to the seller. He and his partner had known that going in—they'd recognized all the risks—but had proceeded anyway.

There was too much upside to getting this right.

So far things had gone smoother than he'd expected and he was regularly the cranky bastard of the two of them. He'd spent his life in New York, figuring out ways to outrun and outsmart the cops, but he'd never once considered the water as their blessing in disguise.

More, it was their ticket to moving the biggest cache of heroin into New York and on through the eastern seaboard.

If they could figure this out, they'd be invincible.

Forget the various mobs who controlled the city. They were amateur thugs who'd bow to Dutch and Mark when they figured this out.

Dutch's excitement beat in his chest as he burned out the last digit. They had it figured out. They just needed to perfect their tactics.

The marks they'd lured for the test runs in the kayaks had worked like a charm. And the news coming out of their leak at the NYPD was promising. She said that the heroin stashes in each of the safes had everyone upside down and confused.

Which was exactly what Dutch wanted.

He'd had to push hard to stash those kilos in the safes—Mark was notoriously cheap—but you had to lose some money to make it and those kilos were a small price to pay for their proof of concept actually working.

Which was why he'd already shifted tactics with the fourth safe, in place and just waiting to be found.

Because it was time to move on to stage two.

His father had been a magician all during Dutch's growing up. His old man hadn't been all that great at the magic routine—he had a simple patter and knew enough to get basic work—but Dutch had learned at an early age that the ability to distract was an illusionist's best friend.

He'd simply taken the technique and built on it until he was a pro. And hoo boy had he put that skill to good use, figuring out the best distraction of them all.

The cops had eyes all over the city. And Dutch had made it his mission to get every damn one of them looking the other way. He also had the added benefit of tying up some loose ends.

Win followed by freaking win.

He stripped off the heavy work gloves he'd used with the soldering iron and pulled a fresh pair of plastic ones from a nearby box. Once fitted in place, he picked up the large envelope he'd meticulously prepared earlier.

Tucking it into the open mouth of the safe, he smiled to himself.

It was showtime.

Chapter 5

Wyatt followed the protocols his department had established years ago and continued to refine over time as he worked his way around the base of the Brooklyn Bridge.

The beautiful landmark was old and while he wasn't an architect in any way, he did keep an eye to any structural abnormalities they'd need to voice backup to the Department of Transportation.

But what he really kept his eye to was the possibility of a threat.

The waters around the bridges were heavily patrolled, along with his team's regular review of their safety, but the NYPD kept a steady and firm focus on the routes that kept New Yorkers on the move. A surprise attack on one of those points connecting the city would signal catastrophe.

The world we live in, his mother would chide and shake her head on the rare occasions when she talked to him about what he did.

Occasions that had gotten rarer and rarer over the past few years.

What did it say about a man who found it easier to avoid his mother than stew in the resentment her home and her life churned up?

Probably the same thing his behavior in the diner said.

For all his attempts at charm, he consistently handled the painful things of his past with a prickly response and an all-around jerky demeanor.

A situation that sat squarely on him when it came to his mother and brother and now with Marlowe, too.

It had been a steady weight since yesterday morning and it had to stop.

God, why did it always turn weird and ugly when any hint of his father's life or Wyatt's own childhood bubbled up?

Marlowe was only making conversation. Moving that getting-to-know-you ball back and forth across the conversational lines that people on a date tossed to each other.

And he'd been enjoying it. He'd been enjoying her. She was bright and fun and challenging and their morning had been going even better than he'd anticipated.

Until he fouled it up with all the emotions he never seemed to get fully under control.

"Yo, Wyatt." His comms echoed in his ear and all those roiling thoughts vanished, firmly pushed to the back of his mind as he responded to Gavin Hayes's call.

"What's up, Gavin?"

Gav's voice was garbled around his breathing apparatus, but Wyatt got the picture all the same. "Got something over here. Twenty yards from the northwestern base."

Since Wyatt was covering the southwestern base it was a matter of swimming a few dozen yards to meet up with Gavin. Recognizing his voice would be equally garbled around his own mouthpiece, he used minimal words to announce his presence. "Left flank."

The water was cloudy and murky—when wasn't it?—but Gavin's high-powered lights filled the space around them, illuminating shapes as well as the silt floor of the harbor beneath them.

"You find something?" Wyatt asked the question, even as dread formed a hard knot in his stomach.

"Not on the bridge." Gavin shook his head as he waved him closer, pointing toward a small black box nestled in the silt about six feet from the base of the bridge. "I think we've got another one of your safes."

They were hardly his safes, but Wyatt got Gav's point all the same. "You touch it?"

Another head shake. "Called you first."

Wyatt kept his breath steady and even, working his way through the shot of adrenaline from their discovery.

Despite his comments to Marlowe the day before, he hated bridge duty. He recognized the importance of the work but he loathed the constant reminder of why they had to do what they did. The never-ending external threats. The lone wolf nuts who had a god complex. The extremists determined to make a point.

It all coalesced underneath the work, a constant reminder of where he chose to make his home and the risks he and his fellow NYPD members all took every day fighting the unending, faceless threats to the city he loved.

To the country he loved.

He'd made his peace with that years ago when he signed on for the job. And he'd recognized that it was his love for his home and his belief in the importance of safety and law and order that he wasn't just called to this job, but he'd chosen it, too.

Yet despite it all, some cases still troubled him. Made him question his fellow humans.

The small black safe—so like the three others they'd pulled to the surface—was one of those cases.

He supposed he should be grateful this one wasn't attached to a body, but it was small solace as he was forced to question if this one actually did have explosives in it.

Were the bodies up to now just to lull them into a false sense of security? And was a bomb really the end game all along?

He gave some quick directions to Gavin before extending his hands for the safe. He did some quick movements over the top, feeling for anything out of the ordinary, but other than the absence of an attached body, this didn't look much different from the other safes they'd brought into the precinct for review.

"Bomb?" Gavin asked.

"Can't rule it out." He shook his head before adding a few orders.

As the more senior member of the dive, Wyatt directed the next steps on the recovery. He'd manage the safe himself, but he sent Gavin on to the surface first to alert the team to what Wyatt was bringing up and to get the bomb squad on their way. Once he had the confirmation from the Zodiac boat up above that the new team had joined them, he'd start his ascent with the safe.

While the other safes hadn't held bombs, it was entirely possible they'd been used to set this all up, distracting everyone's attention off the real endgame.

Especially with the drugs that had been stashed inside.

The only other possibility was this safe had been attached to a kayaker, too. One who'd figured out they were expendable and had ditched the safe before they could risk being taken down with it.

But Wyatt refused to assume anything.

Even if the idea of diving around incendiary devices had images of his father's face coming to mind.

Shaking it off—those ghosts had zero place in his head when he dived—he focused on the problem at hand. With the steady calm that was not only needed in his line of work but absolutely necessary in scuba, he controlled his breathing and waited for the order to ascend to the surface.

They'd deal with this, he reminded himself. Whatever was in the safe, they'd handle it and add to the detective work already in progress, whatever it was they discovered.

He knew he and Gav would be back down here searching for a possible body as soon as the bomb squad took the safe.

When the comms came down from the surface that the team had arrived, Wyatt began his ascent.

And acknowledged the mystery of these locked boxes that kept finding their way into his waters was far from over.

Marlowe evaluated the contact points on the safe she was testing and considered her approach through the small hole she'd drilled with the aid of her pin camera. She hooked three of the wires leading to the lock, clamping them before lightly tugging them through the small opening she'd drilled.

And cursed a streak of blue when she heard the pins of the locking mechanism slam into place behind the door panel.

She stepped back, tossing the grease pencil she'd used to write notes on the door of the safe, the thin snap of the wood against her office floor little solace at the fact that she'd wasted an hour of work.

And had nothing to show for it.

Where had her head gone today?

She'd expected a challenge when she'd agreed to test this round of lock improvements for one of the safe companies she regularly worked with.

But damn it, she was a professional.

One who'd allowed the thoughts rolling around in her head like loose marbles to upset her rhythm and flow.

Which only had a few more choice words erupting from her throat.

How about if we forget about it and put that one in the category of "when I know you better"?

It had been two days since her run and breakfast with Wyatt and she was no closer to puzzling through her feelings about the morning they'd spent together. For all her inward complaining up to now over the man, she certainly had enjoyed spending time with him.

Had enjoyed even more the not-so-subtle sparks of attraction that hummed between them. Their race through the park, pushing each other forward as they ran. The lingering glances over breakfast.

And that kiss.

It had been simple—likely the impulse of a moment—but it had packed a punch.

More than any kiss she could remember in a while.

A long while, she amended to herself.

Although she usually locked the front door of her shop when she was working, the signal for the bell pulled her out of her musings. Goodness she was out of it if she'd forgotten something as simple as locking up when she was going into her office to work.

She mentally chided herself as she wove her way through the various floor safes as well as her worktable in her office before moving into the outer, decorated front area where she welcomed visitors. She kept meaning to hire help but week passed into week, month into month, and she still hadn't done it.

And abstractly wondered if she'd conjured up Wyatt Trumball as she came face-to-face with him, standing just inside the front door.

"Wyatt."

"Marlowe." He nodded, his expression grim as he stood there.

"What's wrong?"

"We found another safe."

She moved forward before realizing the action, her

hand already outstretched toward his forearm. "Oh, no, another body?"

"No." He shook his head, his glance distracted as it floated around the various locks and safes she had on display around the storefront before returning to settle on her.

"Oh, good." At the clear signs of agitation, she added, "Right?"

"That's what's so strange. We're not sure."

"Was there something else inside of it?"

"We're not sure there, either. Bomb squad confirmed there aren't any explosives, but we need to get inside of this one, too."

Although she was glad to see him, she was confused at the reason for his visit. Had he come over just to request her services in opening the safe? Anything she ever handled for the police came via a call, not a personal visit.

Then she keyed into the energy that seemed to surround him like a live wire.

Marlowe had observed Wyatt's calm, logical demeanor as he'd spoken to her grandfather. She also knew his reputation around the 86th, her involvement with the NYPD as well as the connection between her family and the precinct ensuring she knew much of what went on there.

Wyatt was calm and cool and very little ruffled him.

Which was at direct odds with the man standing before her.

"Why don't you come back into my office? Let me just clean up what I was working on." She took the few extra moments to lock the front door and turn the open sign to closed before ushering Wyatt to the back.

"Can I get you something to drink?"

"No, I'm good, thanks."

She crossed to the small fridge she kept in the corner of the office, giving herself a few more moments as well as him time to settle, snagging a water for herself and, at the last minute, one for Wyatt. When she handed it over, he took it with a small smile. "Thank you."

"You're welcome. Now," she said and gestured for him to take a seat on the large stool on the opposite side of her worktable. "Why don't you tell me what's going on?" Before he could say anything, she added, "Whatever you're able to tell me is fine."

He cracked open the water and took a long sip, reinforcing her instinct to grab him one, before setting down the bottle and refocusing on her. "We found the safe on our dive."

"The bridge dive you mentioned?"

"The same. The safe was nestled near the base of the Brooklyn Bridge."

She heard her own gasp and set down her water, unopened. "How'd it get there?"

"We have no idea. And since there's no bomb the standard concerns about terrorism aren't in play. They're not gone," he added, "but they aren't top priority. Especially when you take into account the three safes already recovered."

"It's still an odd place to put a safe. And I can't imagine an easy task, either? I realize you dive that area for a sad reason, but are the waters around it ever really empty of patrol?"

"No." He shook his head, a rueful smile tilting his lips. "But it's not like that water's easy to see through, either. If you had the right motivation and came in farther away, you could navigate under the water potentially unseen."

Marlowe had thought it before but with Wyatt's confirmation she had to admit there were way more facets to his job than might appear at first. The tactical work, the rescues, the fighting criminal activity.

He packed an awful lot into his job and he did it all several feet beneath the water.

"If you need me to come into the precinct I can take a look at it."

"I'd like that. The captain wants you on this from now on. Anything we find, he said, is yours to handle. If you want the job."

"Sure I do. You know I'm always available to offer my services."

When he didn't even come back with a snappy retort about her highly paid services, she finally gave in and pressed him.

"Wyatt, what's really going on? You look like a cat who has jumped out of its skin after getting a bucket of water dumped on it. And while I appreciate the in-person service as well as the job offer, you didn't need to make a special visit for that. And—" She broke off before giving in to the upsetting thoughts that had kept her company for the better part of forty-eight hours. "And the way we left things the other morning had me thinking you didn't want to see me again."

"It's not that." He took the cap off his water and took another long sip, seeming to collect himself. "Really, it's not. And I owe you an apology for the other morning."

"You don't—"

Before she could get the rest of her dismissal out, he leaned forward across the counter, his gaze direct.

Unwavering.

"Yes, I do. I don't talk about my family but I usually have a better handle on how I respond to questions. The emotional check-out routine wasn't fair of me and I'm sorry." He hesitated for the briefest of moments before adding, "And even fumbling like a stupid jerk, I would like to see you again. Assuming I didn't ruin a chance for another morning run in the park or maybe even a date. You know, one with tablecloths and a menu that doesn't look like it's been chewed by a junkyard dog."

Once again, she was struck by how quick he was to not just apologize, but to come off like he actually meant it.

"I'd like that. Although, for the record, those pancakes were pretty great, scarred Formica table and chewed-up menu aside."

"They were pretty great but the company was better."

"Wyatt—"

His name hung there between them and Marlowe lost sight of what she wanted to say, that heavy-lidded gaze going a long way toward making her forget herself.

Even as the reality of both why he was there and why he'd shut down the other day hadn't gone away.

"I realize up until the past few days I've been a bit... prickly with you. But I do know what it is to have a challenging home life. I'm happy to listen if you need an ear. And, well, I'm a vault." She looked around her office with a rueful smile. "Chosen profession aside."

He seemed to consider her, a sort of sizing up that belied the usual interest she saw in his gaze.

But it was still a surprise when he began speaking.

"To your question the other morning, my father was a diver. One of the best."

She heard the past tense but opted to remain quiet, giving him the room to tell his story.

"He was one of the divers called out to the wreck of the Luxair jumbo jet that went down off the coast of Long Island almost twenty years ago."

Marlowe remembered that time. Although she was young, the news of the jet going down, mere miles from its take off at Kennedy Airport, had dominated the local news. "That was the one they thought might be a terror attack, right?"

"They'd thought that as well as any number of conspiracy theories, coming so soon after nine-eleven. But in the end, it was the sad reality of an overlooked fuel problem and a spark from a short circuit that set off a terrible chain of events."

Marlowe felt the involuntary shudder down her spine. She'd always loved travel, but it was never fully lost on her that she was willingly putting herself into a contained tube of metal that hurtled through the sky.

Morose? Yeah, a bit, she acknowledged.

But true? Still a very big yes.

"Your father dived the wreckage?"

"He did. He was one of the first ones called in, his skills widely known and respected. He'd dived the waters off Long Island his entire life. He knew the waters and he knew the terrain. And even he couldn't fully prepare himself for the work or the horror of diving a wreck at that scale."

She listened as he described the hellish conditions

below the surface. The cold, horrible gray environment, with the jagged metal of the fuselage, the risk of pressurized airplane parts exploding if mishandled and, of course, the horrors of all the bodies trapped beneath the surface.

It took a special person to do that, Marlowe recognized. The same sort of person her grandfather was, spending his life working to right humanity's terrible wrongs.

And still, it was something to imagine the work Wyatt's father had faced at the bottom of the Atlantic Ocean.

"He took on the job, going down there day after day and doing his best to bring dignity to all those people who lost their lives."

"That's an amazing thing he did."

"He lost his life because of it. About three days before they were finally ready to pull one of the largest pieces of the wreckage up. He was working with the crew to attach the various cables and he cut himself. He got tangled in some of the wreckage and wasn't able to escape the sharp edges."

She watched as Wyatt fumbled with his now-empty bottle of water. With quiet movements, she cracked her own bottle and handed it over, giving him the space to gather his thoughts as he gulped down nearly half the bottle.

"The team tried to get to him, thinking they could at least share their air, but he was trapped in the tangled wreckage and they couldn't reach him."

"Oh, Wyatt."

He shook his head as he finished what was left in

the bottle. "Even if they had gotten to him, they were much too far down and probably couldn't have gotten him to the surface in time."

He stared at something on the back wall of her office, somewhere over her shoulder.

Marlowe wanted to comfort him, but recognized there was more than the expanse of her worktable between them. There were years and memories and something that felt unfinished hovering in the depths of his dark gaze.

"I am sorry, but I also know those words feel much too small and far too empty to really mean anything."

His gaze returned to hers, a little less lost, less haunted. "They're not meaningless, Marlowe."

Maybe they were and maybe they weren't, but in his retelling she realized there were so many things she wanted to know. Top of that list was how he lived with the reality of his father's death and still do the same work for his own living.

And a very close second was why he'd chosen to tell her.

To trust her with that emotional weight.

"Can I ask you something?"

"Sure."

"I'm not sorry you told me this. Any of this, so please take my question for what it is." When he only nodded, she pressed on. "Why tell me now? Did something happen on your dive? I can't imagine your father's death is something that leaves you, but I'd also imagine that after all this time it doesn't trigger quite this easily, either."

It was a risk asking. Emotional trauma had a way of sneaking up on a person, but that didn't mean they could accurately or meaningfully explain it when those fierce claws took you in their grip.

Hell, she'd learned that lesson long ago.

And yet…she was still curious. Was still full of enough questions to take the chance he might shut back down.

Forty-eight hours ago she was convinced any of the tentative steps toward attraction that had existed between them had effectively ended.

But now?

Now he was here, baring his soul all while requesting her work services.

What was the catalyst?

What did he find on that dive that had churned up emotions he clearly chose to keep buried?

Chapter 6

Wyatt couldn't stop the churning in his gut or the subtle trembling in his body that kept tripping through his nerve endings. It had been this way, off and on, since he'd gotten home yesterday after the dive.

After bringing the safe to the surface and handing it off to the bomb squad, he and Gavin had descended into the waters once more. They did two more dives after that and even with the extra focus they'd been unable to find a body. It was a reality he should have been grateful for, but all he could muster up was a mounting sense of unease.

One he couldn't run off in two loops around the park last evening.

One that was barely assuaged when the feedback finally came just after ten this morning from the bomb squad that the safe didn't hold any incendiary devices.

Even his complaining that it had taken them nearly eighteen hours to get the confirmation had fallen flat, a problem at a warehouse in Queens taking the full attention of the bomb squad and putting that as a priority above his safe.

Which had left him with that increasing unease and an odd, swirling need to see Marlowe.

To make things right for how he'd ended their date.

And, strangely enough, to share the story of his father's death.

He hadn't deliberately come to her shop with any intention beyond seeing her, asking for her help with the safe and apologizing for being so distant at breakfast.

Only the story of his father had come spilling out.

Now that it had, he had oddly settled, those strange trip wires under his skin finally calming.

Even with that leveling out, he couldn't deny her question. He'd already checked out on her once and he refused to do it again.

"No, my father's death isn't usually so raw for me. Or triggered so easily. He's been on my mind, this time of year always bringing back the memories of losing him. And—" He stilled, wanting to get this right. "And I hadn't realized just how close to the surface those memories were until we talked about my family the other morning."

"I'm sorry I asked."

"You don't need to be. It's on me. And, to be honest, it's given me a bit of perspective I didn't realize I'd lost."

That admission cost him, a sign that the happy facade he was always so determined to keep in place wasn't infallible. But in the admission Wyatt also saw another truth: the sky wasn't falling because he admitted to a moment of vulnerability.

He also discovered that he could talk about his father without it taking the strange, resentful overtones it normally took when the subject came up with his mother and brother.

Hadn't that been the difference between him and his brother? Where Charlie had enmeshed himself in anything that didn't have the trappings of dive work or a career that helped others, Wyatt had taken the opposite path. His brother was conquering boardrooms from one end of Manhattan to the other, with Paris, Dubai and Hong Kong on his regular list of travel destinations, all while Wyatt hadn't moved more than thirty miles from where they grew up.

Charlie, just like their mother, had taken the large settlement from Matt Trumball's life-ending dive and put it to use advancing themselves, both professionally and socially. Wyatt had bought a half-decent apartment and left the rest of his money to sit in savings, damned sure he wouldn't forget the memory of his father in the trappings of wealth.

"It's hard sometimes. How grief can lie in wait, leaving you to think you've got it handled before it whips out and reminds you it's still rather firmly in charge."

In Marlowe's words, Wyatt heard something that went beyond comfort. Beyond support.

He heard understanding.

And was once again reminded that while she might still have both parents living, that didn't mean there wasn't pain and that grief she spoke of in the relationship.

For all he and his mother didn't see eye to eye, Jessica Trumball Daniels had used a phrase for years.

Death isn't always the worst outcome.

He'd always thought it callous of her, but seeing the ghosts in Marlowe's eyes, he had to admit his mother had a point.

"I suppose that's truer than we want to admit."

His words lingered as silence once again hovered between them, but he also couldn't deny how nice it was to sit here with her. To sit with a woman he found attractive and not feel he needed to fill the air with lighthearted humor.

That he could be something more.

Sure, he could be a man who did find humor in the everyday but also a person with pockets of sadness in his life. One who could admit that and still be okay.

"I'm glad you shared that with me. That you trusted me with it. But I still get the sense that something else is bothering you."

"This dive. The safes." He shook his head. "I can't get a handle on why they frustrate me so much. Cases are rarely cut and dry and it takes a hell of a lot of work to get through them. And yet—"

He broke off, trying to find the right words for what he'd not been able to reconcile in his own mind. About this case and the emotions he was usually able to keep a tight grip on.

But Marlowe's gentle smile caught him up, stilling that frustration and softening it into something manageable.

"You were diving the waters around New York City

looking for bombs, Wyatt. From where I'm standing your job is about a whole lot of bother."

"That's one way to look at it."

"I saw it for years with my grandfather and, in a different way, I even see it with my own work. Living and working in New York is different. The density of how we live. The mix of extreme wealth and extreme poverty and every imaginable level in-between. And those who prey in and among that, every day of every year. I'm not suggesting police work is ever easy, but it sure as hell is something extra here."

"My family doesn't understand why I do it."

"They don't have to understand. They just have to accept your choice."

"They don't do that, either."

She reached across the worktable, laying a hand over his. Her palm was warm, and he was surprised at how such a simple act of comfort made such a difference.

"Then that's their loss, Wyatt. In every way."

Marlowe laid her tools out beside the recovered safe in the precinct conference room and considered the afternoon. Wyatt's arrival at her shop had been a surprise; his discussion of his family and his father's death even more so.

What sort of weight was that to carry through life? The loss of a parent was always heavy, but the tragic way his father had died? It had to leave endless questions. And a never-ending frustration that the outcome could have been different with a fraction of additional safety measures or a piece of metal that had shorn through and settled on the ocean floor a few inches farther away.

It would be maddening, running through those endless scenarios over and over. For anyone, Marlowe considered, but even worse for someone trained in the same profession.

If the only sadness was his father's death it might be something to work through, but there appeared to be a resonating grief on the other side of the accident with the rest of his family. And while Wyatt might not have overtly shared what had come after his father's death, she didn't need any special skill to read the mix of bone-deep anger and resentment at the mention of his family.

It did, however, make a bit more sense knowing how a cop could afford to buy a home in Park Slope with NYPD salaries being what they were.

If Marlowe had to guess, there had been a very large settlement from his father's death. One that had set his family up comfortably. One that had given his mother and brother a choice about their own lives and a path that was far removed from Wyatt's.

Resolved to think on it later, she took stock of her tools and gestured over to the young cop who'd sat at the end of the conference table keeping tabs on all she did. She might be a civilian consultant but the chain of evidence needed to be maintained at all times.

And now that she was set up and ready, it was time to call in Wyatt and the others who were all assigned to this case.

"I'm ready when the team is."

The young man stood at attention near the door, the wide-eyed gaze he'd given her throughout her prep growing even wider as Wyatt walked into the conference room, their captain on his heels.

"Marlowe." Captain Dwayne Reed crossed over to give her a hug.

"Captain Reed." She hugged him back, the man yet another friend of her grandfather and someone she'd grown up knowing.

"You don't have to stand on formality." His eyebrows narrowed over dark eyes, careworn lines creasing his deep brown skin.

"Nonsense. Inside these walls you're Captain Reed." Even if he was Uncle D whenever she saw him on more social terms.

Wyatt stood behind his captain, his hands clasped behind his back. That earlier sense of restlessness in her shop had vanished, replaced with the cool bearing that seemed to define him.

It was fascinating to see the change, but where she'd previously thought that even demeanor bordered on cocky, their conversation had suggested something else. And after she'd seen the pain in his eyes, she was more and more convinced the man she'd believed she knew was something of a facade. Not a lie, per se, but a cover up for the raw emotions and terrible life lessons that had shaped him.

Couldn't she relate?

She was prevented from considering that too deeply as Dwayne shifted their conversation to more social matters. "How's Anderson?"

"Wily as ever," Marlowe said, shaking off the lingering memories of her own parents.

"Don't I know it. I've been meaning to get him out for a meal. I'll give him a call later to do just that."

While she appreciated the social connection, Marlowe was well aware of why they were standing in the conference room and she shifted her attention toward the table. "Your arrival is timely. I just let Officer Preston know that I'm ready to begin whenever your team is."

Dwayne nodded before turning to Wyatt. "This is your show, Detective. Consider me one more deeply curious observer on this case."

"Thank you, Captain." Wyatt moved closer to the table and addressed his fellow officers, who'd moved into the room and filled in the space around the conference table. "Detective Hayes and I were on bridge duty yesterday morning, reviewing the waters around the Brooklyn and Manhattan bridges. Detective Hayes discovered this safe nestled near the northeastern base of the Brooklyn Bridge."

Marlowe listened to him walk through the details of the discovery, how he and his partner handled the dive and their subsequent search for a body based on the similarity of the safe to the open cases currently under investigation. Although she'd heard it all earlier, the official, almost clinical, retelling didn't pack any less of a punch.

What was going on here?

She didn't need her grandfather's stories to know that in a city of eight million people the full spectrum of what humanity was capable of happened on a daily basis. The local news ensured she had a steady diet of the creepy, the odd and the downright criminal.

But the safes were a mystery.

They weren't large enough to hold much, yet they were tied to so many unknowns.

And death.

An involuntary shudder gripped her at that thought, even as she was silently grateful the safe she was about to open hadn't been strapped to a murder victim.

Wyatt turned from where he addressed the room. "You can begin whenever you're ready, Marlowe."

The evidence team had set up a video camera to record the opening of the safe—more chain of evidence needs—and she addressed the lens as she began to describe what she was doing. Just like the others, her standard masters she always tried first wouldn't unlock the safe. With that determined, she explained for the camera her next steps.

"I can drill into the unit, ultimately bypassing the locking mechanism."

She tapped the face of the safe once more, even though she was familiar with the model and brand. Yet even with that level of knowledge, it wouldn't do to damage whatever was inside. Satisfied she could proceed, she lifted her drill and bore a small diameter hole, still large enough to get her pinhole camera through. If the safe was more complex, she'd have hooked her camera to the room's video feed, but this would be open so quickly it would only waste time so she kept it to her own small screen.

The camera revealed what she'd expected—the inside had been tampered with just enough to negate her master. The pins still locked in but needed her manual work to fully open. With her tools she overrode the lock and felt the door of the safe give.

Stepping back, Marlowe gestured Wyatt forward. "It's all yours."

Light clapping erupted through the room but she kept her face still. Although she stood by her resolve not to look inside, the lingering questions she'd seen in Wyatt's eyes earlier kept her engaged in all that came next.

What was in there?

Drugs had appeared to be the primary motive in all that had come before. Was this another drug run gone bad? Or had someone been transporting the safe and dumped it after getting spooked at a late stage of the game?

Wyatt allowed the evidence team to photograph the interior of the safe as he pulled on a pair of thin gloves, but it was impossible to miss the confused look stamped across his face.

Especially when he finally reached inside and pulled out a thin manila envelope encased in a large plastic bag.

Was this a joke?

Wyatt could feel the small stack of papers inside the envelope and couldn't help but wonder why someone had gone to all the trouble.

"Is that all?" Captain Reed asked from where he stood across the room.

Wyatt gave a quick shake of his head. "I don't understand it, but that's all."

With careful movements, he pulled the papers from the plastic, then unhooked the small brads that kept the envelope closed. Each discarded piece was carefully laid on the conference table as evidence before he pulled out the papers. The stack was small, not more than four pages of printer paper, but what was on the notes seemed so strange.

Someone sank a small safe where they were sure it would be recovered, only to enclose a few photocopies inside?

He scanned each page, puzzling through three photocopies and a fourth page that had minimal writing scrawled across the center of the blank page in heavy black marker.

NIGHTWATCH 1995.

Wyatt flipped back to the photocopies. One was of a *New York Times* article on a jewel exhibit at the Museum of Natural History. The second was for a parking ticket issued in 1995, the numbers that made up the license plate detail smudged to the point it wasn't legible. And one diner receipt from a place in Brooklyn that, based on the address, wasn't there any longer.

What the hell was this?

He handed over the pages to the forensics team, their movements as gentle as Wyatt had been as they settled each piece down on the conference room table to photograph from every angle imaginable.

He glanced over at Marlowe but she'd stepped back, clearly ceding the space to the cops. Her attention was focused on him, not on the activity happening at the table.

But her raised eyebrows and mouthed, "That sure is a surprise," had him moving closer.

Marlowe gestured toward the table. "If I can just get back in there to retrieve my tools I can get going."

"You don't have to leave."

"Yeah, I probably do. It looks like you've got a bigger mystery on your hands than you expected." She shook her head, her gaze drifting to the table. "An envelope? That's really all there was?"

"With a few sheets of paper inside that make no sense and are dated from 1995."

Something flashed in her dark gaze at the date reference but it was gone so fast, Wyatt wasn't entirely sure he'd seen anything.

"Were the victims who were strapped to the safes even that old?"

It was an interesting angle and he was impressed she'd leaped there so quickly. "They were alive, but all would have been children nearly three decades ago. So it feels like a stretch to think there's an overt connection."

"Is it at all possible it's just a coincidence?"

He couldn't quite hold back the grin at that one. After the severe tension of the past few days, he was surprised to realize just how good it felt to smile. "I'm a cop. Do you think I actually believe in those?"

Her smile was swift and immediate, a little zing of understanding arcing between them. "Yeah. My grandfather has never been a big believer in them either."

And that acknowledgment reminded him yet again, Marlowe McCoy might be a civilian, but she had the genes of a cop.

"I'll help you gather up your tools but would you mind waiting for me?"

Once again, something flashed in her gaze he couldn't quite capture before it vanished. "Of course. I'll be in the lobby. Take your time."

He handed her the various items she'd used—the small hand drill, the long thin metal instrument with a hook on the end she'd used in the drill hole, and the small video screen for the pinhole camera that nestled into a padded pouch—and in moments she had slipped out of the room.

The forensics team continued to work with the evidence and Wyatt made his way over to his captain.

"Any theories?" Dwayne asked, his voice low.

"Not a damn one. And each clue we get is more confusing than the last. That's deliberate." Wyatt gestured in the direction of the safe. "A manila envelope with random photocopies inside?"

"Oh, it's definitely deliberate. And it's got a gamelike quality I don't appreciate." Dwayne crossed his arms. "The murders are frustrating enough but now a little game of Clue on top of it?" The man shook his head. "Damn infuriating if I'm honest."

A game was exactly what it felt like, Wyatt thought. He spent a considerable amount of his active training working on strategies to stop criminals. Some were simply dumb and thug-like in their approach to life, the same qualities that made them willing to commit crime making them somewhat more straightforward to catch, as well.

But he had worked cases in the past that never fit the open-and-shut profile. Ones that didn't have the same rhythm or flow of a run-of-the-mill thug on the loose. These cases had more layers to them, and oddly, more finesse. Those criminals not only thought they were above the law, but would like nothing more than to keep the cops running in circles while they did their criminal deeds.

This case had those marked overtones.

It was puzzling and strange and obviously dangerous, but with that taunting aspect underneath.

Seemingly unlinked victims who went down with the first three safes.

Questionable amounts of heroin discovered inside each safe. Nothing miniscule but not exactly a major drug bust, either.

And now this. A trail of unlinked clues he and his fellow officers would have to go on a goose chase to pursue.

News clippings and diner receipts?

A hell of a lot of nonsense they'd spend time on while missing out on taking the needed next steps to reach the endgame.

Their forensics lead set down her camera and gestured them both over. "We're going to take all of this, but as soon as I get to my computer I'll email you the images so you can start digging into this. The information's not clear on all pieces, which my gut tells me is deliberate."

Wyatt nodded. "I'll keep you posted but for the record, I don't think you're wrong there."

"We'll get the handwritten note into the lab and see if we can get any better sense of the pen used or the paper or even if someone slipped and included a fingerprint. We'll let you know."

"Thanks."

The woman rounded up her team and filed out, leaving Wyatt, Dwayne and Gavin in the room.

"It's a hell of a thing," Gavin started in once the room had cleared. "And what is Nightwatch?"

"Hell if I know," Dwayne said, a mix of disgust and puzzlement coloring his tone. "And I was on the squad in ninety-five. Nothing rings a bell."

"We'll check the files," Wyatt said. "See if we can find anything or any reference. I'm not sure if the date's a help or something to throw us off the scent but we'll start in the mid-90s and work our way forward and backward from there."

Dwayne was quick to provide his support. "Let me know how it goes and if you need more help on this. Seems like your dive skills are at a premium right now."

His captain looked Wyatt straight in the eyes before giving Gavin an equally serious once over. "Be careful down there."

"Yes, Captain," they said in unison.

"I'll leave you both to your evening, then." Dwayne left the room, the weight of their work riding his shoulders as much—if not more, Wyatt thought—than his own.

"I'm going to get a head start on this Nightwatch stuff."

"Take a look but knock off at a decent time. We're down again tomorrow and the captain's right. We can't lose focus on our dives."

"You got it."

Wyatt watched him go and once again considered the weight on Dwayne's shoulders.

The load that bore down on all of them.

And wondered, yet again, what madness they were up against.

Chapter 7

Marlowe waited on a small bench near the front of the precinct. It had been a surprise to realize just how much time they'd spent in the conference room and it was nearly seven when she'd finally taken a seat, settling her tools beside her.

Settling in to wait for Wyatt.

It was an oddly cozy moment and she fought to keep her head about her. She wasn't a woman made for cozy moments or domesticity. Her background had ensured as much. Yet the more time she spent in Wyatt's company the more she wondered if she could be made for that.

For the bond that kept two people in each other's orbit, day in and day out. Sharing space. Sharing a life.

The deep thought was far too intense for someone

she'd had a pie date with that had also included her grandfather and a second date over a run and breakfast. Yet the thought remained all the same.

She was intrigued.

And with the intrigue came the addition of that flutter low in the belly that spoke of anticipation and need. Two things that left her vulnerable and wide open to hurt.

Worse, the vulnerability opened her to the potential for deception.

Did she ever want to be in that place again?

A dating relationship was hardly the same as parental family bonds, but she'd lived with the reality of betrayal. Of what it meant to put your hopes on someone who wasn't worthy of them.

And it hadn't just been her father. He might have done the work of a criminal but her mother's reaction to Michael McCoy's thievery and deception was to abort ship and emotionally abandon her child in the process.

It had only been her grandfather who had provided a safe harbor.

Anderson McCoy had done his very best, but none of it could fully make up for that betrayal.

Could anything, ever?

Even as she knew that for truth, she had to admit Wyatt hadn't had an easy time of things, either. It wasn't a competition—no one wanted to play "who had the worst childhood?"—but he had lived with pain, too.

And if she'd read between the lines, that pain had followed him into adulthood, just like her.

"Those look like some serious thoughts for a late summer evening."

She glanced up out of those serious thoughts that never felt too far from the surface to find Wyatt. He'd changed out of his slacks and dress shirt that had an NYPD logo in the corner to a pair of jeans and a gray T-shirt that had the word "Brooklyn" emblazoned across that always impressive chest. A few weeks before she'd have looked at him and disdainfully thought "frat boy" and mentally moved on.

After, of course, she admired that impressive chest.

But now that they'd spent time together, she recognized the flirty, nonserious behavior she'd always associated with him was a bit of diversion. Not the sleight of hand her father was best at, but something of a protective layer Wyatt wrapped around himself.

"There's lots of serious to think about," she finally said.

"Want to go out and find some of the less serious?"

"I'd like that."

He took her work bag without being asked and headed for the exit. Marlowe didn't even muster up an argument. The bag was heavy and it was nice to share the load.

But she did keep pace beside him as they both said good-night to the guard on front desk duty before walking out into the pretty September evening. The sun was low in the sky, backlighting the street in front of the precinct in a reddish gold hue, the last rays of sun filtering through the three- and four-story buildings that made up the block.

"I love September in New York."

His agreement was immediate. "It's the best. Still warm but not oppressive. And some of the prettiest sunsets over the water you'll ever see."

"What's your favorite time of the year to dive?"

"As long as there isn't a hurricane coming in, right now's pretty nice. All summer, really. Even with the layered suits, the job is a lot less enjoyable in winter when it's stone-cold freezing."

"I'll bet."

They talked off and on about the intricacies of his work before coming to Baker's Pub. It was a newer entrant in Sunset Bay's young professional renaissance and she had only been here once with a group of friends.

"This work?" He nodded toward the bar and the lively sounds spilling out to the street.

"This is great. Though I am a bit surprised."

"Oh?" Wyatt pulled the door open for her, more of that happy, lively noise greeting them.

"I'd have thought you'd take me down to Yancy's."

"You want to go to a cop bar?"

She shrugged. "I figured that's where we were headed."

His grin was swift and once again, caught her hard at the knees.

"What's that smile for?"

Wyatt gestured her into the bar. "You've got the bug and you want to talk about the case. Maybe some hard-boiled detective talk over a few beers?"

"Don't you want to talk about it?"

He leaned in beside her, his voice nearly a purr in her ear. "I want to talk to you. If the case happens to come up in the course of conversation, so be it. I have zero interest, however, in hanging out with a bunch of cops."

They were heady words and her earlier thoughts of cozying up to Wyatt had a pedestrian sort of sweetness that had nothing to do with the shots of desire that speared down her spine before radiating out through her body like a sparkler. With his hand low on her back—sending out more of those sparks—she wove her way toward an empty booth on the far side of the room.

Wyatt gently deposited her work bag on his side of the booth before sitting.

"Thank you for that."

He glanced up as he reached for the menus stuffed against the side wall. "For what?"

"For not tossing my bag into the seat before you."

A small line creased the space between his eyebrows. "You have expensive equipment. And even if you had feathers in there, it's not my bag to toss around, gorilla style."

"Thanks all the same."

He let whatever he was about to say drop as a waiter came up to them. After he'd departed with their drink and appetizer orders, Wyatt once again focused on her.

"Now it's my turn to thank you. For the help today. For waiting around." He quieted before continuing on. "For listening earlier at your shop. I appreciate it."

Although she avoided speaking of her parents with anyone other than her grandfather, Marlowe realized a small offering was more than fair. "It's so hard to lose a loved one. But what comes after? That's hard, too.

"And it's difficult to realize your parents aren't who you thought they are. Or maybe better said, who you hoped they were."

"Even if those are the hopes of a child?"

Wyatt's face drew up in serious lines and once again, Marlowe recognized something there in his relationship with his mother. Something that had struck an incredibly deep well of disappointment.

"Becoming an adult doesn't change our family bonds. I don't think we ever lose our need for our parents." She hesitated, before adding, "I never did."

He nodded at that but didn't say anything further. Yet despite the quiet, Marlowe got the distinct sense they'd gained another layer of understanding between them.

Even as she was grateful she didn't have to tread her own personal scorched earth and talk about her parents.

Maybe she'd be ready at some point, but not tonight.

"Thanks as well for taking on the safe work for this case. You're a pro, Ms. McCoy."

"They're puzzles and I love solving them. Locks. Combinations. Even where to drill. It's a perpetual challenge."

"You had a lot of safes in your office." His gaze narrowed. "And I was so busy talking I didn't even ask any questions earlier at your shop. You had a lot of tools laid out on your work table. Were you working on something when I interrupted?"

"You didn't interrupt. In fact, you provided a very welcome diversion from a puzzle that was not revealing any clues to me."

At his ready interest, she added, "I regularly test new offerings for various safe companies. I have running contracts with several of them to test their products, give suggestions and discuss weak points."

"You really are a badass safecracker."

"I prefer lock and vault technician." She aimed for a serious demeanor, but it rapidly dissolved into amusement. "But yeah, I'm a badass safecracker."

"How'd you get into it?"

"That love of puzzles again. And too much time on my hands one summer as a kid."

She considered telling him more—how that summer she'd played with every lock in the very large house by the ocean her parents had taken her to. It was one of the more idyllic summers of her childhood, even if it had been lonely. It was in the time before the world knew the depths of her father's crimes and, if her mother had known of them, had still looked the other way, pretending they didn't exist.

Pretending the glamorous life they were living was funded in some way other than through theft.

That summer had also provided endless challenges to a kid left alone for far too much of it.

"Sounds like a lot of kid ingenuity," he said.

If Wyatt sensed there was more to her story than a summer of modest mischief, he ignored it.

Biding his time? Or had she just gotten that good in breezing through her background that it was as commonplace to her as breathing?

The questions—and their vastly different answers—faded as Wyatt continued.

"Whatever way you developed the skill, the NYPD is certainly grateful for your talents. I'm grateful for your talents."

Marlowe reached across the table, the move as instinctual as it was natural, and laid a hand over his. "What you do, Wyatt. It's not easy. I never thought it was but seeing this case up close? It's reminded me that police work isn't just hard, it's all-consuming. There's no laying it down when the day is over and walking away."

Once a cop, always a cop. It got in the blood.

He'd said as much the evening he'd taken her home after talking with her grandfather, and in those words Marlowe recognized the truth.

"Maybe not," he said, turning his hand over beneath hers, "but there is something to be said for taking some enjoyment at the end of a hard day. Let's do that."

As she looked at him across the table she saw the weight of the case on his shoulders. But she also saw the willingness to set it aside for a bit.

How could she deny him that?

Why would she even want to?

Wyatt took the last, satisfying bite of his burger, and marveled at the evening. He'd asked her to stick around after she'd completed her work in the precinct conference room because he wasn't ready to say good-bye. The off-kilter way he'd left her after their break-fast, followed by the unnerved retelling of his father's death in her shop had left questions in his mind and he'd wanted a bit of time alone with her to see if she'd already written him off.

To his delight, she not only hadn't written him off but was an engaged, enjoyable dinner companion.

Or maybe, dumbass, your instincts were right and she was one of the few people you could actually talk to about your father.

It wasn't a particularly enlightened thought, but it did have merit. Especially because he spent so much of his time trying to avoid the topic that not talking about it had grown a bit heavy in his mind.

He also recognized a kindred spirit in her acceptance

of his life experiences. He hadn't told many women he'd dated the specifics about his father's death, but it did come up from time to time. Any relationship that progressed to something even moderately serious included discussion of family, parents at the top of that list.

He'd always received compassion when he'd spoken of his father's death, but he hadn't always sensed that deeper layer of understanding.

Because while she might not be living with the death of a parent, Marlowe lost her father as surely as he lost his. It was clear in her understanding and in all the things she didn't say.

Even her story of how she got interested in her work smacked of sadness and a sort of lonely existence he'd sensed.

And then somehow—miraculously—she managed that conversational magic that seemed to be her stock-in-trade and made him forget about his family and his maudlin thoughts entirely.

"Okay, so I told you the strangest thing I've ever pulled out of a safe. It's your turn. Weirdest thing you ever pulled up on a dive."

"Weird weird or gross weird?"

"Either." Her eyes lit up. "No, actually, how about both?"

"Okay, so gross weird is body parts."

Marlowe settled her burger down. "Do I really want to hear this?"

"You asked!"

"Fair." She smiled and picked up her burger. "Have at it."

"To be honest, you probably don't want full details.

But I will say it's a more persistent aspect to the job than I'd ever expected."

"But you do body retrieval."

"Yes," Wyatt agreed, "which was what I expected. It's the body *part* retrieval I wasn't quite ready for. My first year on the team we pulled up four severed hands, quite a few fingers and a body part every man would prefer to have left on him, even in death."

"Oh." Her mouth formed a small O. "Oh, wow."

"Yeah. Fortunately that was a one-time thing." He laughed in spite of himself. "Rookies are already given a hard time. I was the butt of a lot of jokes for about six months after that one."

"Okay. Fascinated though I am, I would like to finish this really outstanding burger. So tell me about the weird weird."

"Doll heads."

"Well, yeah, they're part of the creepy hat trick for a reason."

"Creepy hat trick?"

"Doll heads, clowns and little twin girls with pigtails and matching dresses standing at the end of a long hallway. They're classics for a reason." Marlowe popped a fry into her mouth. "Where did you find these doll heads?"

"We had an evidence retrieval up in Spuyten Duyvil."

"And equally creepy place since it's Dutch for the Devil's Whirlpool."

"You're good."

"I love my New York history and there's no lack of it here. But that's got to be pretty hard to dive. Those waters were named that for a reason. And—" She broke off, a pretty blush covering her cheeks. "I'll stop now since I'm talking like a walking encyclopedia."

Her knowledge of their home was a pleasure he'd never expected. "I was actually thinking what a lovely dinner companion you are."

That heightened color remained, even as she smiled. "Then I'll keep going with my questions. Because those are tough waters, aren't they?"

"Most of New York is with how the Hudson River meets the Atlantic Ocean."

"Is it hard to dive?"

He considered her question and the speed with which she zeroed in on an aspect of his work. "Diving's never easy. There's a lot of training involved for a reason and you can't forget where you are or what you're doing. But yes, working the waters around the city has additional challenges based on time of day, the tides and the overall mass of humanity and boat traffic in and around the waters."

"You always dive in teams, though?"

"We do."

A strange expression came over her face and he couldn't resist pressing her. "What is it?"

"Never mind." Marlowe shook her head. "It's dumb."

"You can't lead with that and not tell me."

"What about sharks?"

Now that was a question he got a lot. The whole team did and he knew the public fascination with sharks made for an easy way to talk about what he did—or divert from the less public aspects of the work.

"They're a part of the job and we do see them from time to time."

Marlowe's gaze narrowed. "How often is time to time? And how can you be so casual about it?"

"I'm not—" Wyatt broke off and reached for his beer. "Okay, so I am a little casual. But we work around them. They're more active at dawn and around dusk so we try to avoid those times for our routine work. Helping victims in an emergency will always take precedence, but for our standard surveillance work we avoid them."

"Okay, that's one way."

"We also dive in pairs so we can keep watch for each other and we avoid getting near any situation that looks like they're feeding."

"It still seems like a risk."

"What I do is a risk. But believe it or not, there's a lot more risk dealing with criminals than marine life. Sharks really just aren't that interested in what we're doing. And if you add on the Zodiac boat is following us and there's crew keeping watch there to alert us if we need to surface it's not a big source of difficulty."

"Color me unconvinced." Marlowe smiled as she reached for her glass of wine. "But then again, I watch *Jaws* religiously every year over Memorial Day weekend so maybe I'm a bit influenced by that."

"To your point about the dollheads, it's a classic for a reason."

She toyed with the stem of her wineglass. "What you're really saying, though, is that the sharks on land give you a lot more trouble than the ones in the water."

"I guess I am."

"And those notes today? In the safe?"

"We'll handle it. The forensics team will do their part

and we'll start running down the information on each page."

"It seems like a lot of running around."

He eyed her over the rim of his beer. "You sure you don't want to try out for a job on the force? That was the exact conversation I had with Captain Reed after you left. It feels like a decoy of some sort and a deliberate waste of everyone's time."

"It's an awful elaborate trick."

He was already replaying his conversation with Dwayne and Gavin in his mind when Marlowe's comment stuck a hard landing. "Trick?"

"Well, yeah. First you have the murders and the fact the safes were strapped to someone. Any way you look at that it's a significant crime all by itself. Then you put a fourth safe in a place where it's sure to be discovered by a dive team?" She tapped a finger on the table. "You said the other morning that the regular dive checks aren't public knowledge. Not truly public or just something that's not publicized?"

"The latter. Our presence in the harbor isn't a secret. And the remit of my team isn't a secret, either."

"Which means someone went to a whole lot of trouble to put a standard-sized valuables safe at the base of the Brooklyn Bridge. Something that could have easily gotten them caught and in a heap of trouble."

"Yeah."

"What's the endgame? Because it's like they're doing it backward. Killing people only to then bury a safe with some photocopies in it? It's backward. Wouldn't you work up to killing people?"

"You'd give your grandfather a run for his money."

That smile was back, even brighter than before and without a trace of her earlier bashfulness. "That man lives, sleeps and breathes casework. I've heard him talk about his work my whole life. Clearly some of it sunk in by osmosis."

"But you are right. Murder is a sad outcome, but it is often an endgame. Not the place a criminal begins."

"Which leaves the bigger question. What's the real endgame here?"

Dutch answered the burner phone in his pocket and his contact on the other end wasted no time in sharing an update.

"The cops got it. You can consider the package received."

He debated how much he wanted to ask—paid-off marks were notoriously tricky—but he wanted an answer.

An answer would dictate the next step.

"Safe's in evidence?"

"Yep. Contents, too."

"McCoy do the work?"

"She's the only one they're using on these jobs."

It was an interesting development and one he hadn't been able to plan for. But Marlowe McCoy's reputation preceded her. Locksmiths might be a dime a dozen but one who could genuinely crack safes was another story.

When that safe cracking came with the McCoy pedigree, it was like catnip and comfort for the cops, all rolled into one.

And it made his work that much more satisfying.

"So the payment?" his contact asked, her voice shifting toward anxious for the first time.

"It'll be where we discussed."

"Now?"

He avoided sighing and instead pushed a smile into his tone. "In place and ready for you to pick it up."

She mumbled a quiet thank-you and ended the call and Dutch sat there for a long while, considering the mark. She'd been an ideal choice, her ex-husband's gambling problem ensuring there wasn't any money left over to pay for child support. She needed the cash, but he knew the work didn't sit well with her.

That light quaver in the voice always told the truth.

And payoffs to those who were desperate never worked quite as well as those in it just for the money.

He had a few more safes planned but would cut her loose as soon as the work wrapped.

And hoped like hell there didn't end up being a need to take her out.

Chapter 8

Marlowe glanced around the elegant midtown restaurant and wondered why she was here.

Curiosity?

Personal amusement?

Or was it that persistent childhood need for her mother's approval, even when she'd never receive it?

Sadly, she knew it was the last.

It was always the last, no matter how badly she wished she were able to find some sort of smooth, cool detachment from the relationship.

Her mother's call and surprise announcement—that she was in town from Arizona and could they meet for lunch?—had come in while Marlowe was at dinner with Wyatt. The light, airy happiness that had followed her into her apartment after dinner had vanished when she'd listened to the message.

Her mother had traveled more than two thousand miles and hadn't bothered to mention it until she was already here?

Marlowe had lived with Patty McCoy's dreamlike disposition so long she shouldn't be surprised but, like it or not, she could still be flustered.

Damn it, no. She could still be mad and hurt and emotionally wrecked.

And wasn't this the problem with cozy?

With those flutters in the belly?

Something always waited in the wings to snatch it all out from underneath you.

Although she didn't know her mother's reason for visiting, there was some discussion her father's parole hearing would be moved up from the following spring to this October. And while her parents were long-since divorced, anything that involved Michael McCoy always involved his ex-wife.

If for no other reason than Patty loved the drama. Even the whole "finding herself in Arizona" smacked of a rather large sense of self-involvement and dramatic license on how to explain away the poor decisions of her life.

"Darling!" Her mother's greeting—part coo, part cry for attention—echoed from four tables away.

Marlowe waited for her mother's arrival and considered the woman she hadn't seen in three years.

The long, flowing blond hair was a bit more platinum than Marlowe remembered, but still worn in that long, straight bohemian style her mother favored. Her skirts were flowy and her bracelets jangled, but that clink was most definitely eighteen-carat gold.

No roadside crafts or hammered bronze for her mother.

She might have perfected the boho look, but it was tinged with the distinct signs of wealth.

Wealth that had come only from the riches of others, no matter how Patty had managed to spin that truth to herself.

Their embrace was surprisingly warm and her mother held on a bit tighter than Marlowe expected before pulling back. "Darling. How are you?"

"I'm good, Mom. What about you? And what a happy surprise you're here."

"I love New York in September and I realized I was well overdue for a visit."

"Where are you staying?"

One gold-wrapped wrist jangled in a casual brush off. "I got a hotel in the city. Thought I'd get a bit of sightseeing in while I was here."

Marlowe would be the first to call her relationship with her mother strained, but they were cordial to one another. And while it might have been years since their last visit, whenever Patty came east she always stayed with Marlowe in Brooklyn.

All this only added to the underlying questions about the impromptu visit.

Settling into their seats, Marlowe recognized the only way to understand what was going on was to let things play out, however Patty ultimately chose to work up to it. But by the time she walked out of the restaurant, all would be revealed.

They ordered lunch and fell into simple conversation over sparkling water and mixed green salads. Her mother's careful questions about Anderson and Marlowe's work carried a practiced air.

"You're still doing your lockwork?"

"Lock, safe, vault management. Yes, all of it."

"I still can't believe there's enough work in that to make a living."

Marlowe hesitated to tell her mother that her business had cleared more than a half million dollars the prior year. Or that she was currently contracted with three safe companies in addition to the private work and the consulting jobs she did. She was proud of her work, but it didn't matter to her mother.

Because Marlowe hadn't taken a traditional "female" job, nor had she found a husband to take care of her.

For all the suggestion of casual independence the bohemian look implied, her mother was shockingly traditional. Antiquated, even.

"There's plenty of work."

"Yes, well." Patty let that hang there before continuing on. "Have you spoken to your father?"

"I visited him back in July. That's the last I've seen or spoken to him." Marlowe took a sip of her sparkling water, her question casual when she finally spoke. "You?"

"Last week. Michael believes his parole hearing will be moved up and that he'll be out before Christmas. Wearing one of those horrid ankle bracelets if he gets out." Patty shuddered. "But away from that wretched place."

"He's serving his debt to society, Mom. Those in charge expect it to be paid in full, whether he's in or out of prison."

"As if he's some common criminal."

"He is a common criminal."

They were hard words but they'd gotten easier over the years. It had been a fantasy to think her father wasn't "like the other prisoners." That his code of ethics—sketchy though they might be—elevated him out of the garden-variety criminal category.

Only time and acceptance had helped Marlowe recognize the truth.

Her father had dedicated his life to stealing from others. Her mother could delude herself that his behavior somehow elevated him from murderers and rapists, but the law didn't.

And Marlowe had long since gotten past her anger about that.

Sadness, yes.

But anger or fury? That was nothing but wasted emotion when it came to her father.

"Well, it will still be good to know he's not rotting in a cell."

"Who knew you cared that much?" Marlowe chose her words carefully, but even she realized the small talk and the charade of ignorance had gone on long enough.

"I've always cared, Marlowe. You know that. It's because I cared so much I had to move away. Had to get away from the knowledge my husband was in that horrid place."

"Apologies if my violin isn't in easy reach."

"Don't you sit there casting judgment on me. Your father wasn't the only one who lost his freedom the day that sentence came down. I lost my life."

"Your life of lies."

It was old ground but her mother had never doubled down quite so hard, either.

Which was the first inkling something more was going on. Smoothing her napkin, Marlowe settled back in her chair. "What's really prompted this visit?"

"I've met someone."

"Oh. Oh, wow." Whatever she'd been expecting that wasn't it. Although she wasn't naïve enough to think her mother—a single, unattached divorcée—didn't date, Patty had always had a quality that had suggested she wasn't fully over Michael McCoy, either.

It was subtle—a sort of longing for an earlier time—but had always been somewhat distinct. And a clear roadblock to finding her own happiness.

"Well, that's great for you. Really, Mom. I'm happy for you."

At her acknowledgment, Patty smiled her first real smile since they'd sat down.

"His name's Brock and he retired to Arizona about three years ago from California."

Patty spent the rest of their salads and most of their entrées detailing the wonders of her new relationship. How she and Brock met, their active social life and the fact that she believed he was going to ask her to marry him.

"I'm glad you found each other."

"Yes, well—" Patty broke off. "It's your father I'm worried about."

"I hardly think Dad would stand in your way. He's only ever wanted your happiness."

"Maybe so, but, well… Brock doesn't know about your father. And he can't find out."

"You're lying to him?"

"It's an omission, which is hardly the same thing. And why would I risk running him off?"

It was as if a cold bucket of water had been dumped over the top of her head and all Marlowe could do was sputter. "You claim to love him."

"I do love him."

"So be honest with him."

"My ex-husband is a convict. That's not liable to go over well with a man who's done quite well for himself in life and currently serves on three boards in his retirement."

So there it was.

That distinct sense of self-preservation that had always lived beneath the dreamy, airy facade Patty showed the world.

That self-defense had allowed her to ignore the realities of her husband's life for more than twenty years of marriage.

The same self-delusion had allowed her to believe walking away from her child, leaving her to fend for herself, would all be okay in the end.

"If you want to enter the bond of marriage under that cloud, that's your call. What does any of this have to do with me?"

"Brock and I are in town. He had some business to conduct and suggested we could meet you for dinner. He'd like to know you."

"And this was the advance show to make sure I didn't spill the beans on dear old Dad."

"I'm asking you to behave with a bit of decorum, Marlowe. That's all."

Decorum?

That's what the kids were calling lying your ass off these days?

Marlowe wanted to say no. Way down deep inside she wanted to walk away and wash her hands of all of it.

But that same little girl who still missed her mother—who still craved her attention and affection—was the only one who managed to find her voice.

"Sure, Mom. I'll go. Just tell me where I need to be."

Wyatt combed the silt beneath his gloved hands and mentally counted off the minutes he had left before his ascent. They were in the Hudson, running an op to recover a weapon, but all he could do was count the minutes until his shift was over.

It was a new sensation. He loved being in the water, and he loved what he did. But even Wyatt recognized the current mystery they were dealing with was firmly on land.

What was it with those sheets of paper? And why would anyone go to all that trouble?

It'd been three days since Marlowe opened the safe they'd discovered under the Brooklyn Bridge and still not a single clue had been unearthed from the strange documentation discovered inside.

A *New York Times* article? While interesting, a review of that case had turned up nothing in the archives. There hadn't been any crimes reported in or around the museum and nothing about the exhibit featured in the article.

A diner receipt and a parking ticket? Nothing to find on either of those.

And what the hell was Nightwatch?

Endless questions, with no answers.

He continued with the diving exercise, returning his focus to the evidence they were trying to run down. A report had come in just as he'd gone on shift that there was a fight on one of the ferry crossings that morning. Said fight had ultimately resulted in a switchblade being pulled, and then subsequently tossed overboard when security came to break up the fight.

The fact that the switchblade had also damaged internal organs on the victim had put Wyatt and his dive partner on the hunt for evidence. He was diving with Kerrigan Doyle this morning and while they hadn't been partnered often, he was incredibly pleased to see her progress. She'd been with the team for about two and a half years and was a strong, focused diver.

The alert on his comms unit that she'd found the knife only added to his positive impressions of the young woman.

Damn, she was good.

And because she'd found the knife so fast and they were in a fairly shallow depth, they could ascend without any concerns.

Moving in close and tapping her on the foot to alert her to his presence, he signaled his intention to head up and got her thumbs-up in return. She'd already put the knife in an evidence container and begun her ascent, as well. They reached the Zodiac one after the other and they waited while Amos took the container and stowed it before helping Kerrigan and Wyatt into the boat.

Free of his breathing apparatus, Wyatt tilted his head

towards the evidence. "Great job, Kerrigan. That was a fast find."

Kerrigan glanced up from where she settled her oxygen tank in the Zodiac. "I got lucky, but I'll take it. Of course, luck may not be the exact right word. I did manage to get a handful of dead rat first before landing on the knife."

She was unnecessarily modest, but with the rolled eyes and moue of disgust, Wyatt couldn't help but laugh. Unfortunately, the disgusting aspects of the job were something they could all relate to.

Unbidden, Wyatt remembered his conversation at the bar with Marlowe. Although she had teased him, he hadn't missed how fascinated she was by the things they often pulled up out of the water. "Funny enough, the subject of the less appealing things we pull up off the seafloor was dinner conversation for me the other night."

"Aren't you the sparkling conversationalist, Trumball," Kerrigan teased him.

"I heard it was more than dinner," Amos said with a smile, all too anxious to get in the conversation. "I heard you were out with Marlowe McCoy."

Wyatt was careful with his answer but he wasn't going to deny it. "She's helping with the safes we keep dragging off the harbor floor."

"Yeah, yeah, it was just a casual thank-you dinner. At Baker's no less." Amos waved a hand. "I realize the woman grew up around cops, but those are some pretty rank sweet nothings you're whispering at the great

Anderson McCoy's granddaughter. If you're gonna romance her, where's your game, Wyatt?"

Marlowe McCoy's not a game.

The words were nearly out of his mouth when he snatched them back. Both because he had no interest in being the center of gossip and more because he felt the congenial facade that usually carried him through any manner of work conversations fading hard and fast from some harmless ribbing on Amos's part.

"It was a few drinks and burgers."

Amos shot Kerrigan a knowing eye but seemed to recognize it was time to shut up.

And with it, Wyatt tried to get out of his damn head. Date or not, he had been out with Anderson McCoy's granddaughter. The whole evening could have been perfectly innocent and they'd have been the center of gossip.

The fact he was interested…

He'd better figure out a way to handle it around the rest of the team because people were going to talk.

The call came in, alerting them to a new problem and forcing the worries about gossip to the back of his mind.

Amos picked up the radio, answering even as Wyatt and Kerrigan sat and waited for what would inevitably be new direction and a new set of orders.

"You got it," Amos said. "We're close enough to follow in the Zodiac and my officers have second tanks with them. Estimated arrival three minutes."

Wyatt and Kerrigan began checking equipment, reviewing the two fresh tanks they'd already stowed in the Zodiac in anticipation of a possible second dive on the knife retrieval. Amos signaled to the larger NYPD boat they worked with and followed as soon as the larger boat was in motion.

"We're headed to Chelsea Piers," Amos hollered over the sound of the engine. "Tourist in the water."

Wyatt muttered a curse before hollering back. "Alive?"

"Dispatch says yes."

"Then let's aim to keep it that way."

Kerrigan settled in beside Wyatt as Amos maneuvered them out of the harbor and up the Hudson River. She pointed to the evidence container still attached in the far corner of the Zodiac. "I guess I should consider it lucky I found the knife already."

"Damn fine work, Doyle."

Kerrigan shook her head in seriousness, but it was hard to miss the sarcasm in her voice, even over the high-pitched whine of the engine. "Could've been even quicker if it hadn't been for the damn rat."

Wyatt was grateful for the laugh as they helped each other with their tanks, getting set into position. The joke was also enough to diffuse the lingering tension from the good-natured ribbing over his date with Marlowe.

Because it had been a date.

In the days since their evening at Baker's, he'd tried to convince himself otherwise, but even he knew better.

The department might be talking about him and Marlowe, but gossip ran in the halls of the 86th like fresh-flowing water. And when he wasn't the subject of any of it, he rode those currents with as much pleasure as the next person.

So he had no right to get touchy about it now.

As Chelsea Piers came into view, activity abundantly clear up against the waterfront, Wyatt put it out of his mind.

Even if he did vow to call Marlowe tonight and ask her out again.

Marlowe prided herself on being a levelheaded woman. She took responsibility for her actions and for her life. It was a simple detail she knew and understood about herself and it had absolutely no bearing—nor was it a help—on the wildly raging emotions she had experienced for the better part of seventy-two hours.

Had she and Wyatt gone on a date?

Were they going to go on another date?

And was she actually contemplating inviting him into the ridiculous charade with her mother?

Even if it did feel a bit like getting an ally on her side for what would inevitably be one of the most awkward evenings of her life.

"Get the hell out of your own head," she muttered as she logged into her email after being out on a job site all morning. "Find something productive to do. Even I'm sick of myself."

It wasn't like she and Wyatt hadn't spoken or that he'd pulled a jerk move and ghosted her. In fact, it was the opposite. He'd texted every day since she'd last seen him and he'd called one evening to see how she was doing. He'd asked her on another morning park run for the following week, his schedule of morning shifts this week interfering with his morning runs.

He was mature.

Honest.

Open and transparent.

And she was torn between asking him to commit social subterfuge or pulling a jackrabbit and walking away from the man like a quivering lump of fear.

What the ever-loving hell, McCoy?

Since she'd just opened ten emails and hadn't read any of them, she took a deep breath and tried a new tack.

She might have agreed to meet her mother's new boyfriend but she didn't have to go. There were a million excuses she could make up and likely a few that weren't even BS. What she needed was to think through what she really wanted to do.

Lie, which sat uncomfortably on her shoulders.

Chicken out of the evening, even if it only solved the problem for a short while.

Or decide if it was time to take the more nuclear option and cut her mother out of her life.

Since all options sucked she refocused on her computer, surprised to see an email from her father's lawyer as she continued to scroll through what had come in. The email held the details of her father's upcoming parole hearing—now moved up to late October—with information about the case under review included.

There'd been a time when she'd cared deeply about her father's case, but it had been years since she'd even bothered to do an online search. The details had consumed her when she was younger, but in time she'd come to realize that the endless combing through articles had no bearing on her life.

None of them were fully accurate portrayals of the man she knew.

Nor were they entirely inaccurate about how he spent his life and how he'd ended up caught for a crime he'd committed. One that had come after a long line of crimes he'd also committed yet escaped any consequence.

With the case number noted in the email she did log into a search program, curious to see how the facts matched her memory.

The case details were heavy on the legalese but she read through the specifics and knew they were as damning as she remembered. The heist of a downtown Manhattan loft, purported to hold art to rival a museum. Her father had set his sights on a small sculpture and an exceedingly rare bronze that had been worked in Florence during the Renaissance.

He'd nearly gotten away with it, too. But a recently installed video camera on the building across the street from the loft, as well as a telling confession from a known associate who was looking to cut his own deal on a different crime, had been enough to put her father away.

More curious than she wanted to admit, she pulled up a fresh search bar and typed in the name of the known associate.

Harry Kisco.

The search returned several pages of info, but she clicked on the images option first, curious to see if she recognized the man who'd put her father away. Shots that had clearly come from outside a courthouse showed a big man with his arm up, hiding from the camera. A scroll farther down the page finally turned up a mug shot some enterprising reporter had included in a story.

Did she know him?

Had he been a part of her parents' social circle?

Her mind drifted back to the story she'd told Wyatt of how she'd first gotten interested in locks. Was it possible Harry Kisco was there, that summer in the Hamptons when she'd spent hour after hour alone in the big rambling house with the locks and the picks she'd found in a drawer and an old library with a big safe in the wall?

They were old memories but she really didn't think she recognized the man in the photos.

She'd nearly closed out of the search program, aware that this was not only a pointless waste of time, but likely a dumpster diving exercise tied to the situation with her mother.

Way too many emotions churning up old memories.

"Put it away, McCoy. Get up. Clear your head." She'd nearly done just that when her gaze caught on an image at the bottom of the page.

The man she'd been looking at—Harry Kisco—stood with his arm around another man, photographed in front of a nightclub. The logo on his shirt caught her attention before she realized it was a match for the branding on the sign behind them.

Nightwatch.

She clicked on the image and quickly read the caption underneath.

Harry Kisco and partner, Mark Stone, launch new Brooklyn nightclub, Nightwatch, in Williamsburg.

Nightwatch?

Although she hadn't been privy to the information coming out of the safe in the precinct conference room, she had seen the oversize writing on one of the sheets of paper Wyatt pulled out of the business-sized envelope.

NIGHTWATCH 1995 it had said.

What was one of her father's known associates doing with information that matched evidence coming out of the safes from the harbor?

Her exchange with Wyatt as they'd left the 86th whipped back into her thoughts, a distinct echo of the questions now roiling in her mind at the image of the two men and their nightclub.

Is it at all possible it's just a coincidence?

I'm a cop. Do you think I actually believe in those?

Yeah. My grandfather has never been a big believer in them, either.

Coincidences.

Any way she played it, there wasn't a single scenario she could muster up where this was an accident of fate.

But what to do about it? She could ask her grandfather but she wanted to respect Wyatt's work. And if she hadn't been standing on the perimeter of the conference room she'd never have seen the scrawled note anyway.

But she had.

And now she had an odd, albeit tenuous, connection to her father?

The date of his parole hearing was coming up. Would this ruin his chances of getting consideration for early release?

A heavy knock echoed from the front of her shop and she crossed out of her office and into the reception area, ready to send whoever was there away.

And came face-to-face with Wyatt, standing on the other side of the glass door.

Chapter 9

For the second time that week, Wyatt stood outside Marlowe's shop, the need to talk to her overriding his natural inclination to simply text.

It felt like a bit of overkill but he'd already intended to ask her out and the rescue at Chelsea Piers had ended up being more intense than he'd anticipated. What had started out as a standard water rescue had turned into a bigger issue when the husband of the woman who'd fallen overboard decided to go in after his wife. While a deeply moving gesture, the man hadn't anticipated the height of the pier or the shock of the water and Wyatt and Kerrigan had needed to split their efforts against two people along with the rest of the rescue crew.

And tough rescue or not, you just want to see her, Trumball.

Which made it that much more startling when he caught sight of her face, starkly serious, through the door of the shop.

He'd already come to understand she wasn't a woman of easy emotions. It fascinated him more than he'd have expected, but in moments like this he had to admit that depth could be jarring, as well.

Was she okay?

Marlowe opened the door and stepped back to let him in, but before he could lean closer to press a kiss to her cheek she stepped out of range.

Deliberately?

Wyatt recognized the broader truth—they didn't know each other that well, despite the obvious interest that sparked between them—and he opted to give her a bit of space and see if they'd come far enough that she'd trust him with whatever was bothering her.

And if she didn't?

Wyatt mentally shrugged it off. He'd worry about that later.

"I hope you don't mind I came straight over. I was going to text you but went on impulse once my shift wrapped up."

"Okay day?"

"It was challenging, but successful, so I'll take it." He watched as she played with a small card rack on the counter, straightening the rectangular shape so it was even with the counter edge. "I thought you might be up for another evening out, but it looks like I might have caught you at a bad time."

Her gaze shot up at that. "Why? I mean, why do you think that?"

"You seem distracted. Busy. I can take a raincheck."

"That's probably better. My mother made a surprise visit to town and she wants me to meet her and her new boyfriend for dinner. So another night would work."

Wyatt nearly left it at that but something in the way she described the impending dinner with her mother— or perhaps the subtle frown that wasn't typically part of her demeanor—clued him in.

"You don't want to go?"

"I—" She let out a small sigh. "I wish it were as easy as that."

"I have a few minutes. You did a damn fine job listening to my family drama the other day. If you want to talk about it, I can lend an ear."

It was hard to miss the struggle stamped across her face. And as someone who kept their family life exceedingly private, Wyatt understood her challenge to open up.

To share details that—when spoken to another— forced acknowledgement they even existed.

But her small smile that broke through the clouds ultimately made him glad he asked.

"Why don't you come back to my office? It seems to have the right ambiance for family confessions."

Once settled, funny enough in the same spots they'd sat the other day for his own retelling, Marlowe recounted the unexpected arrival of her mother into town.

"We don't have a great relationship but she does stay with me when she comes to town so that was my first clue something was off. But when she began telling me about Brock it sort of made sense. And then she dropped the bomb on me about lying about my father."

"What does she want you to say?"

"She wants me to omit any mention of him or the fact he's spent the better part of over ten years in prison upstate."

"Are you going to go?"

"Unless I can come up with a better excuse than rearranging my sock drawer, I'm not sure I can get out of it. And I hate being this weak."

Marlowe dropped her head into her hands before seeming to think better of it, her spine straightening until she looked about to shatter.

"I'm in charge of my life. I work hard, I own my own business. Damn it, I'm not a pushover. But with her—" She broke off, misery stamped across her physical form like a brand. "With her it's like I'm twelve again and I crave her approval in the worst way."

"Without putting too fine a point on it, of course you do. It's your mom."

"It's ridiculous. She's ridiculous." Marlowe stopped, then stilled as those words hung between them. "That's unkind. But I keep circling around that description and can't seem to come up with a better one.

"She sat there all excited about this new man in her life and how she hopes to marry him. And in practically the next breath she's telling me how we're going to simply omit the truth of the past years of our lives. Hell, the reality of her marriage, whether she knew what my father was up to or not."

"Did she know?"

"I've asked myself that for years and the answer never changes. I just don't know. At the end, yeah, of course she did. But before then? Before he got himself in too deep?" Marlowe shook her head. "I think she found a way to delude herself so that she never looked too hard under that rock."

It was oddly cathartic to hear Marlowe recount those experiences and even more, humbling to realize he saw traces of his own relationship with his mother in the absurdity of Marlowe's retelling.

While he'd always believed his parents had a love match, his mother never made a secret of her fears for his father and what risks he took as a professional diver. And when he ultimately took on the Luxair job and lost his life because of it, his mother had been all-too-ready to take the very large legal settlement and move on.

Move on past their modest home and solidly middle-class existence and into the wealth his father's death had perversely bequeathed to them.

He'd spent a long time being angry about it, but now faced with Marlowe's experiences, he recognized the layers of anger were far more nuanced. Yes, they were threaded with grief, but they also held resentment, disappointment and that sense, even if rather subtle, of disgust at how easily Jessica Trumball had moved on.

From their family life.

From the memories of her marriage.

And, in less than two years, into a new marriage with someone who was most definitely not his father.

He'd spent a long time feeling guilty about that and maybe he needed to cut himself a break. Especially since he didn't hold Marlowe accountable for her mother's actions.

Or her poor decisions.

"You're not weak, Marlowe. You're the furthest from weak I can possibly imagine."

She wanted to believe him. Oh, how she desperately wanted to believe in the gentle kindness and subtle strength Wyatt offered.

But how?

She was seriously contemplating endorsing this ridiculous scheme of her mother's. And now she had this strange, coincidental clue about her father and the case Wyatt was working and she was keeping it to herself.

For all her inward self-aggrandizing that she was a woman of honor and conviction, it had taken a shockingly quick holiday at the point of having something to hide.

Or potentially hide.

Which only added to the confusion. Was it because she was reticent to tell him about that weird, tenuous connection to her father? Or did it just feel like a bigger deal than it really was because she was keeping it close to the vest?

And all in the face of him being so warm and considerate and, as she was fast coming to understand, just Wyatt.

"Thank you for saying that."

"You don't sound like you believe me."

"I'll work on that part."

Maybe she would after she got a handle on this whole business with her father's known associates. She hadn't even gotten a chance to look further into the two men who were in that photo. And she needed to call her father and follow up on his parole hearing.

Michael McCoy had never been forthcoming with her about his former life, but if she worked her way into the conversation with him she might be able to get some information.

Then she could tell Wyatt.

After she understood what they were possibly up against.

Because coincidence or not, what would a long-gone, nearly thirty-year-old nightclub have to do with dead bodies and safes in the harbor? And could she dare risk her father's parole hearing on something that might be nothing?

Wyatt slipped off the stool on the other side of her worktable and moved around the room. He stopped before a large biometric safe she'd been tinkering with over the past few days, an upgrade to the software part of a series of tests she was running for the manufacturer.

"Is this one of the safes you mentioned working on and trying to crack?" He tapped the large front door, currently bolted shut.

Reluctantly, she let the imagined conversation with her father go. She'd do a deeper dive into those two men and see what she could find as a search engine detective. Then she'd call her father. And then she could tell Wyatt what she knew, no matter how important or inconsequential.

"It is. That's a top-of-the-line biometric safe. They've made continuous upgrades since bringing it to market and wanted me to try to get through the new protocols."

"How'd you do?"

The laugh came quick and easy and, with it, the realization that she hadn't smiled so naturally since the last time she was in his presence. "Knocked it out in under a minute."

"Ouch." He winced. "Sounds like they need to do a bit more innovating on their side."

"Yes and no." She came around the table to stand beside him. "The basic construction of the safe is unchanged from last year's model so I had a leg up since I already knew how to get in."

"Why not change that up, too?"

"Much as the business is always trying to keep up with criminals there are some things that are just too hard to change. Reengineering an entirely new safe takes time and there's no way to make those sorts of structural changes to the entire line on offer every single year. So there are tweaks. Upgrades. And with the advent of the biometric product offerings, a lot of work software can further support the integrity of the safe."

"Such as?"

His question was simple, but the heady, intense way he looked at her as he asked had those damnably wonderful flutters kick in just below her breastbone.

"This safe for instance," she said, pointing to the electronics panel. "Once installed, this unit will connect into a security system, can record fingerprints for authenticity and there's even an upgrade option for iris recognition."

"So even if someone gets in, they've left a biometric record."

"You bet. It's a game changer. Where safecracking

used to be tied to finding a way in, now it's also about risking what you're going to leave behind."

"But you still got into it in under a minute."

"That's my job."

The vivid blue of his eyes remained steady on her, lightly roaming over her face. She detected his scrutiny, but instead of feeling the need to run, she discovered it only fueled her own hunger to look her fill.

To somehow commit him—to commit this moment—to memory.

The hard lines of his face, chiseled over a solid jaw and a sharp, straight nose. The full lips, almost too much except for the wide, even smile beneath. And those eyes.

God, why did she never remember just how blue they were?

Or how intense it was to have the full interest of his gaze, holding her captive?

It was fanciful and borderline ridiculous, those thoughts, Marlowe acknowledged. Yet as he closed the space between them, his hand moving up to her shoulder as he used his body to press her back to the solid wall of the safe door, she could hardly argue with the overwhelming reality of Wyatt Trumball.

"I think you're entirely too modest about your skills." His voice was a whisper against her lips. "And under a minute is impressive in any field, anywhere."

Before she could muster up a response, his mouth closed over hers, those firm, generous lips coaxing hers open beneath his.

Had she really thought them too full? Marlowe wondered as she opened her mouth beneath the gentle assault, nearly moaning when his tongue swept inside to expertly stroke hers.

The large hand on her shoulder slid down to grip her hip, his fingers gently cupping her flesh as he pressed more directly against her.

This wasn't the quick move in the park or the light kiss they'd shared the night he drove her home from her grandfather's. This was something different.

Hot.

Needy.

All-consuming.

And it had the distinct notes of the inevitable, laced beneath the all-consuming pleasure.

Was sex with Wyatt inevitable?

And had all their flirting and increasing time spent in each other's orbit been about driving to something more?

She wanted it, Marlowe admitted to herself as she ran a hand through the hair at his nape, using gentle pressure to pull him even closer to her. Allowing him to take the kiss even deeper, the carnal pull between them so electric, she was half surprised they didn't manage to set the tech panel on the safe to sparks.

With one last press of his lips, he lifted his head, staring down at her. That vivid blue was hazed with desire but she also saw a spot of mischief.

"Do you need someone to go with you to the dinner?"

"Dinner?"

She was so involved in the kiss the change in topic had her stumbling over the meaning of his question.

Those notes of mischief sparked a bit deeper in his gaze. "With your mother."

"You'd…want to do that?"

"I want to support you. If sitting through that dinner with you helps, then I'm happy to go."

She nodded, the taste of him still so fresh on her lips she couldn't imagine saying no to anything he asked. "I'd like that."

"When is it?"

"When is what?"

"Dinner."

"Tonight. Eight o'clock. In a restaurant in Manhattan. Midtown…" Her voice trailed off. "Steak."

"I'll come get you around seven?"

"Sure. Yes." She tried to focus on his question, even though the feel of his hand still on her hip and the heat of his body pressing fully against her chest had her imagining far more interesting ways they could spend the evening. "Seven sounds good."

Wyatt pressed one last, firm kiss to her lips before stepping back. "I'll pick you up then."

She remained where she was, her back pressed to the safe, slightly worried she didn't have the ability to stand fully on her own yet. So she stayed there, turning her head to watch him go.

It was long moments after he left, her gaze trailing around the room as she weighed the strength in her legs that Marlowe recalled what she'd been doing before he arrived.

Her attention landing on the open lid of her laptop, she remembered the search query still open on the screen. And the lingering questions of whether or not

Wyatt's current case had any possible connection to her father.

On a hard sigh, Marlowe pushed off the safe and crossed to the laptop, snapping the lid into place.

And regretfully acknowledged she might have more in common with her mother than she thought.

Wyatt pulled into the parking garage at the end of the block where he and Marlowe were meeting her mother for dinner. It had been a quiet ride into the city and she hadn't said much.

Which had left Wyatt to replay their earlier kiss over and over in his mind. Not like it had been too far from his thoughts from the moment he'd left her in her shop.

But damn, the woman had gotten beneath his skin.

He was interested, sure. But this deeper need that continued to kick up? It had all the hallmarks of interest and a healthy dose of good old-fashioned lust, but there was something more there. He was a man who trusted his instincts in every way and something about this developing attraction between him and Marlowe was rapidly pushing him out of his comfort zone.

Did he mind?

He chose to ignore that sneaky question as it slipped and slid through his thoughts, crossing around the car to help Marlowe out. But the moment her hand gripped his, those beautiful legs swinging out of the car, he was right back to that place she always managed to send him. Outright fascination and tempting desire.

You're meeting her mother, Trumball.

Meeting.

Her.

Mother.

Tamping down on his hormones, he took the ticket from the valet and reached for her hand.

He didn't normally drive to Manhattan, usually opting for the convenience of a car service, but he didn't want to risk them being late because of a surge in driver demand. And knowing how important this evening was —whether she wanted to admit it or not—Wyatt didn't want to end up forced to take Marlowe into the city on the subway because they were rushed for time, either.

"There it is." Marlowe pointed toward the end of the block. "Marino's Steakhouse."

"It'll be a good meal."

"Sure. Right." She nodded as is psyching herself up. "It'll be great, lying to my potential new stepfather."

"Your mother's doing the lying."

Marlowe shot him a side-eye as they headed for the restaurant. "Wyatt. Whatever we're doing tonight, let's please not pretend I'm not aiding and abetting this whole charade."

"Fair enough." He squeezed her hand. "But before you judge yourself too harshly, why don't you let it ride and see how things play out? Your mother is likely viewing all of this from a point of embarrassment. Use this evening to get a feel for this guy she's seeing and maybe you can gently persuade her to come clean."

He saw the moment his words registered, a distinct softening in her mouth and a brightness filling her gaze. "I hadn't thought about it that way."

"I appreciate how you feel, but I meant what I said.

You've been dragged into this, but it isn't your lie or your relationship. Give her a chance to do right."

It seemed to be the correct sort of pep talk because he saw the distinct relaxation in Marlowe's posture and disposition as they walked into the restaurant. A woman who was clearly her mother, both in build and similar coloring, was hanging on an older gentleman in the lobby of the restaurant and Wyatt did a quick assessment as the tableau played out before him.

The light tinkle of laughter from the woman who practically cooed his name as they were introduced.

The firm handshake of her partner, a man with a booming laugh and slightly self-deprecating air that still never let you forget he was large, rich and in charge.

And finally the gentle hug with barely there kisses against each of Marlowe's cheeks as her mother pulled her close.

Although he hadn't intended to invite himself into her evening with her mother—and up until thirty seconds ago had blamed his reason for being here on his unmitigated and raging hormones for the woman by his side—now that he was here he was glad for it.

More, he recognized it was exactly where he needed to be.

Especially because the older couple who preceded him and Marlowe to their table checked every box Wyatt had been expecting. Patty McCoy might be playing a role, but Brock Abernathy wasn't exactly a slouch.

This only added to his expectation that the guy Marlowe's mother was desperately hoping to make husband number two had already done a rather thorough search of his own on one Patricia McCoy and the background she'd rather forget.

"So Wyatt, Marlowe tells me you're a diver for the NYPD." Their waiter had barely cleared the table from taking their drink order when Patty started in.

"Yes, I am."

"That's fascinating." Brock quickly took over. "How did the two of you meet?"

Patty's face set into slightly pinched lines but Wyatt kept his smile broad and his answers breezy. "Marlowe is one of the NYPD's favored lock and vault technicians. You'd be surprised by how often we have to have a locked piece of evidence unlocked and no one's quicker or more efficient than Marlowe."

Wyatt sensed Patty's relief as the conversation of how they met bypassed Marlowe's connection to the 86th via her grandfather.

"And I guess since Marlowe's a civilian you can date on the job like that?" Brock asked.

Wyatt pumped in the charm, tossing a broad, unrepentant smile at Marlowe before turning back to Brock with a wink. "I didn't ask for permission."

"We've only been on a few dates but I thought it would be fun for us all to get together this evening." Marlowe kept the conversation smoothly moving forward. "And speaking of dates, how did the two of you meet?"

Patty's excited retelling got them through cocktails and appetizers and on into the start of their entrées.

"Wyatt, are you a native New Yorker?" Brock asked as he cut into a steak so rare Wyatt wondered how it wasn't still mooing.

"I am. Born and raised on Long Island before settling in Brooklyn once I joined the NYPD."

"I'm west coast born and bred myself." Brock shook his head. "Never got the appeal of living here."

Well, gee, let me put you in touch with the tourism commission, Wyatt thought. "The city's not for everyone, sir, that's for sure."

"All these people. And all this crime," the older man sputtered as he waved a fork. "The fact you have to have a damn scuba team, for Pete's sake, to keep the city safe. It's madness."

Wyatt didn't quite make the connection. Every denizen of the city could be angelically perfect in their behavior and the NYPD would still need a scuba team. New York City and water were inextricably linked.

"There's no place like New York," Marlowe chimed in. "And to Wyatt's point, the city might not be for everyone. But for those of us who choose to live here, we love it."

"What brought you to Arizona, darling?" Brock turned his attention to Patty, sensing the cold shoulder even if he couldn't quite pinpoint the increasing chill from Wyatt and Marlowe.

"Oh, that's a tale as old as time." Patty waved a hand, even as Wyatt wondered how that particular line of questioning never came up. "I wanted a change after my divorce."

"Right, right. And when was—"

Patty steamrolled through any additional questions with a sweet smile and an added, "Just like you, dear. Sometimes we're just done with a place and want to start over somewhere new."

Whatever else he was, Wyatt was a reader of people. And if these two made it to the altar, he pegged them for two years, tops, on the marriage.

It was one more facet that shed light on Marlowe's life.

Her mother was fine, all things considered. A bit ridiculous, especially with this absurd charade she was perpetrating, but relatively harmless overall.

But she was careless.

It didn't settle very well that he saw strains of his relationship with his own mother, especially since she'd also moved onto her second marriage and the new life that had come with it.

Was it like Marlowe had said earlier?

Were they always destined to seek a parent's approval, regardless of whether or not the parent even deserved to give one?

Because as they sat here, it was evident that Marlowe had to live with the consequences of Patty's selfish streak. One that might be steeped in the woman's own sense of hurt at her ex-husband's actions but which had dire consequence on their child.

For someone who'd spent his adult life avoiding the emotional realities of losing his father as a teenager and all the difficulty that came after, it was jarring to realize how his time with Marlowe had upended it all.

And how quickly the veneer of breezy humor he'd built around himself had cracked, simply by spending time with someone who made him look more deeply inside himself.

Those thoughts kept him company throughout the

rest of the meal, along with the tedium that had set in even before their dessert and coffees were delivered.

"Mom, Brock. It's been a lovely evening, but we should get going. I know Wyatt's got a day of diving tomorrow and I have to be on a job site by eight."

He looked over at Marlowe, only to find her looking right back. And in that moment, he realized they'd spent the entire dinner as partners.

Not the adversaries they'd been up until that evening at her grandfather's.

And not the interested unattached adults who'd been dancing around each other for the past few weeks, trying to figure out their next moves.

But real partners.

He'd come tonight to give her support and ended up humbled that she had his back as much as he had hers.

That feeling carried them out of the restaurant on more air kisses, hearty handshakes and the instruction to meet them the following weekend for a farewell dinner before Patty and Brock flew back to Arizona.

"Whew. That was a whole deal." Marlowe had already tucked her hand in the crook of his arm as they walked back to the parking garage.

"You handled it beautifully."

"Right back at you on that one. But seriously." Marlowe practically danced beside him down the sidewalk as she relayed her impressions of the evening. "What is my mother thinking? He's got the good old boy routine down well but there's ice in those veins. Does she honestly think she's going to keep her past from him?"

And once again, Marlowe proved that subtle sense of

street smarts and a lifetime of training at a cop's knee as Wyatt handed over his ticket to the valet.

"He's already run her. I'll bet you a year of dinners he knows every last detail about your father, including what cellblock he's in."

The post-dinner excitement that had ridden Marlowe's tone dimmed as they waited for the car. "I've no doubt he does. Which doesn't exactly make me feel good about this. I walked in upset with her lack of ethics on this, but can't get over a creeping sense of distaste over his, too."

Wyatt had kept the stub off the ticket while they waited for the valet to bring his car up and handed it over as the man jumped out of the driver's side. The valet had stopped just shy of the sidewalk to allow them to get into the car and Wyatt pulled open the passenger side door.

And immediately shoved Marlowe down, head first into the seat, as the sound of gunshots rang out, echoing off the metal frame of the car in a loud series of pops.

Chapter 10

Marlowe's cheek pressed against the leather of the passenger seat, the heavy sounds that had pierced the air and then into the frame of the car fading away. Wyatt's large body still covered hers from behind and she tried to catch her breath against the heavy, solid weight of him.

"Wyatt." His name came out on a strangled moan and she reached behind her to grab his hand. "Wyatt!" She squeezed, the move enough to have him shifting and giving her a chance to gulp in air.

"Are you okay?"

"I'm fine but you're heavy. I need to breathe."

"Don't move from where you are. The seat's low enough you're covered by the dash. Keep your head down and as low to the floor as you can. I want to check out what's going on."

Hard, unflinching cop lined each and every word that fell from his lips, including the fact that he'd given an order he had every expectation would be obeyed.

But what had happened?

Was this a random act? She lived in a large metropolitan area and knew it wasn't only possible, but it happened to people every day.

Yet even as she considered it, with the sounds of shouts outside the car a steady accompaniment to where she still lay in wait for Wyatt's all clear, she couldn't help but wonder if that was delusional thinking designed to make herself feel better.

Wyatt was working on a major case.

Was it possible this shooting was tied into that and not really random at all?

And if it was, what had Wyatt actually uncovered on the bottom of the harbor?

Even with her grandfather's career on the police force and her father's criminal acts, she'd spent no part of her life with active exposure to violent crime. The idea that it was closer than ever settled into her bones with chilling clarity.

"Marlowe. Come on out." Wyatt's hands were gentle on her shoulders as he helped her up, pulling her from the vehicle. A wholly irrational shot of fear raced through her as she was suddenly free of the car, her body exposed to anyone who might be walking on the street or hiding with a gun pointed right at them.

"Are you sure?"

"It's okay. Cops are here and the area's under watch."

"Watching where? Those shots came out of nowhere."

"They actually came from a nearby office building,

three floors up." He gestured with his head to the area behind them. "A team's already on it and running down all the clues they can find, but the window the shooter was in has been cleared."

It should have made her feel better, especially since they'd run down the origination of shots so quickly, but those lingering questions still filled her thoughts.

Was this deliberate?

And if it was, who was the target?

Who would even know she and Wyatt were headed into the city tonight? Or their exact location and where they parked.

"Is this about the safes?" The question was out before she could stop it, along with a shot of adrenaline that set her teeth chattering as her body processed the overload of fear and shock to the senses.

"The safes?" Wyatt's eyes narrowed as lines creased his forehead. "Why do you ask?"

"It doesn't feel random."

"No, it doesn't," he said before pulling her close against him. That same large form that had pressed against her in her office and then again in protection against the seat, now surrounded her offering comfort.

Protection.

And the promise that she had a safe place to land as her body worked off the rush of hormones that controlled her baser need to fight or flee.

Marlowe leaned into him, burrowing into that sense of safety and security, even as her thoughts continued to toss around like pinballs, scenario after scenario playing through her mind.

Random or deliberate?

A warning or an attempt on their lives?

Was she the target or was Wyatt?

When that adrenaline response flared once more at the idea the shots were directed at Wyatt, Marlowe knew her first real moments of bone-crushing fear.

This thing between them was new—so new they were still fumbling their way through text messages and dates and questing kisses.

Yet it was real.

More real, more quickly, than she could have ever imagined.

The back of a squad car was never very comfortable—and no one really liked knowing they had no way of opening a car door on their own—but Wyatt bit down on his own internal frustrations and kept his focus on Marlowe.

Arlo and another officer from the 86th had shown up about an hour after the gunshots. Wyatt had exhausted any and all leads with the midtown precinct that managed that part of the city and was just about to call for a car service when Arlo had shown up to escort him and Marlowe back to Brooklyn.

There'd been a brief discussion about whether or not to call Anderson but in the end, the fear her grandfather would hear it from someone other than her had Marlowe dialing him at close to midnight.

He hadn't needed any help to piece together Anderson's side of the conversation, the older man's voice ringing loud and clear through the squad car.

"What do you mean shot at?"

"Wyatt and I were in Manhattan, meeting Mom and her date for dinner."

"Your mother?"

"Yes, Pops. She's in town like I told you."

"Are you okay, Lowe?" A hard exhale came through the phone. "Were you hurt?"

"No, Pops. I'm fine. I'm in a squad car now being driven back to Brooklyn and I'm with Wyatt. I'm fine."

Arlo's attention had remained riveted on the conversation, but there was a distinct glance in Wyatt's direction when Marlowe had made mention of spending the evening together.

When all he got was a dark, pointed look from Wyatt he'd turned his attention back to the drive across the bridge into Brooklyn, but Wyatt had no doubt the quelling look hadn't diminished Arlo's attention to the call.

Or his curiosity as to the status of Wyatt's relationship with Marlowe.

"Have the squad car bring you straight to my place."

"Pops, I swear I'm alright. The cops will see me to my door and I'm sure I can even get them to do a full sweep of my apartment. It was a long night and I want my own bed. But I'll come by first thing in the morning."

She'd made several more promises that she was fine and that she'd be by bright and early before disconnecting the call.

"He's worried," Marlowe finally said. "He usually gets a solid dig in at my mother when he's able and the fact he let it slide says he's worried."

"Of course he is. We can still swing by there. I'm sure he's awake."

"No, the morning will be fine. I need to get home and get my morning appointment canceled. I'll head to his place instead of going out first thing on a job."

The squad car maneuvered through Brooklyn, the late hour, on a weekday no less, made it a relatively quick trip back to Park Slope. And then Arlo got out of the squad car and opened the back door for both of them to get out.

"Thanks for the ride."

"We'll wait for you," Arlo said to Wyatt, gesturing toward the front of Marlowe's building.

"No need. I'm staying here."

"Wyatt, you don't—"

Marlowe's protests were already expected and gave Wyatt the time to cut her off. "I'll sleep on the couch, but I'm not leaving you here tonight alone."

She looked about to argue before obviously thinking better of it. But she did give Arlo a stern look. "Let the record show that I argued on this one. Especially when the grapevine at the 86th gets a hold of this."

"Nah, Marlowe, Trumball's right. We'll all feel better if someone's here tonight." He shot Wyatt a dark grin. "I'm happy to volunteer, though."

Arlo ducked out of range before Wyatt could say anything and headed back toward the squad car, a decided spring in his step.

"Sorry he's being an ass."

"I thought it was sweet." She glanced back at her building. "And you really don't have to do this."

"I will be a perfect gentleman and I promise you're not going to become an object of gossip, but I'm not leaving you. And I'll go with you to your grandfather's in the morning."

"Bossy aren't you?" she asked as they walked up to the door of her building.

"When I need to be yeah." He waited until they were inside before he turned to her, laying a hand on her arm. "But this isn't being bossy. This is helping a friend and ensuring you're safe. And since we don't have a firm idea of what happened tonight, I'm sticking close."

Fascinated, he watched as a host of emotions telegraphed from her expressions and physical demeanor. From a frustrated sort of bravado to an aching sadness, he saw it all.

But under it all rested an overwhelming sense of relief.

"Thank you."

He might have been staying, regardless of her agreement to the idea, but was pleased to see her acquiesce without argument. And it added to his own need to take what minimal control over this situation he could find.

They had no idea who shot at them or why. The two of them appeared to be the intended target. Or was it just Marlowe or him? Wyatt had no idea, nor was he even close to a working theory.

He kept circling back to the safes.

But why?

They'd been put into the waters around New York City in a way that would ensure they'd be found. So now they were found and suddenly a faceless problem is taking potshots at cops?

He and his fellow NYPD officers knew they lived

with risk, both in the execution of their job, as well as by virtue of the fact they put on a uniform each day.

But this?

It kept going back to his captain's point when they'd uncovered the papers in the last safe.

It all felt like some sort of game.

Why?

Beyond the fact the press had covered the murders of the kayakers, the precinct had kept the information about the safes on lockdown. And since they'd been sitting on a frustrating lack of leads, he or any of his fellow team members hadn't even done a lot of interviews with potential suspects or even witnesses on the matter.

The information simply wasn't widespread yet.

But if the shots were about the safes, what was someone afraid of?

More of the frustrating, endless arguments that seemed to abound with this case.

"Can I get you anything? Coffee or a glass of water?" Marlowe asked.

Exhaustion rimmed her eyes, a sure sign the adrenaline rush had sparked itself out and left the need for sleep in its wake.

"I can help myself to some water. Why don't you go on to bed? I'll take the couch."

"I can get you some pillows."

He glanced across the small area that made up her living room and pointed to the large blanket on the back of the couch and the colorful throw pillows propped in each corner. "I've got all I need there. Seriously, go on to bed."

She turned into him, pressing her lips to his in a soft

kiss. The temptation for more flared, quick and high, but he held back.

Just like that realization after dinner—that Marlowe had been his partner tonight, in every way—Wyatt understood the needs of this kiss were different than the heated passion that had nearly consumed them in her office. And while he wanted her—and increasingly knew that was the inevitable trajectory between them—he liked being with her, too.

Liked this wonderful variability between comfort and desire.

Even if all he was willing to give tonight was comfort.

Because when the flames of desire spiked enough for them to act, he'd be damned if it was after they were exhausted and vulnerable.

He wanted it to matter. And he wanted them wholly focused on what was between them instead of using sex as a consolation prize.

She meant too much for that.

So it was with a gentle kiss in return that he pulled back. "I'll see you in the morning."

Marlowe blinked at the bright sunlight filtering in through her bedroom window, the events of the previous night slamming back into her thoughts and clearing the dreamy haze of sleep.

Wyatt was here.

Images of the night before kept assaulting her, a driving counterpoint to the oddly dreamless sleep.

He'd ridden home with her in a police car, then insisted on staying. Only instead of putting the adrenaline rush of the prior night to good use, he'd chastely kissed her and sent her off to bed.

What the hell was that about?

Because a man who kissed like the very personification of temptation—and she could still feel the scorch marks of his chest from when he pressed her against the safe in her office—shouldn't be able to turn that off at will.

It was hell on a woman's ego and, well, damn…

The mental tirade ended as she sat up and looked down at her clothes. She'd been so tired last night she hadn't even made it into her pajamas. Instead, she'd fallen facedown into bed in the light wrap dress she'd worn to dinner.

Damn the man, how did he know just the right thing to say and do?

She considered it all while changing into casual clothes and brushing her teeth, vacillating between grateful to annoyed and back again.

Because she was grateful.

He'd come to that farce of a dinner with her and supported her. He'd protected her in the midst of gunshots. And then he'd stayed last night, ensuring her safety and, likely even more important, her peace of mind.

Lingering guilt still remained over her father's known associates and the call she needed to make to him in prison, but she had a plan. And she would tell Wyatt what was going on once she had all the details.

Much as she needed to snip that loose thread, she knew that wasn't what had her so out of sorts.

So why did it suddenly feel like she was losing it as a wholly irrational itch settled under her skin?

Wyatt's protective qualities were great and she appreciated his presence more than she could say, but damn it, why had he rebuffed her kiss last night? She'd been all ready to consider putting sex on the table and he'd sent her off to bed.

Alone.

Without sex on the table. Or at least the proverbial one, though now that she considered it, her table was solid oak and looked fairly sturdy...

Pulling herself back, she got irritated all over again. Damn his honorable tendencies and the whole protecting her and sending her off to bed.

The damn fool man.

Marlowe padded out of the bedroom and found him, already up and playing on his phone from his position on the couch. She also smelled fresh coffee, which meant he'd been up long enough to do that, too.

"Good morning." Wyatt looked up from his phone. "Is it?"

"You tell me." He grinned, seemingly unfazed by her grumpy, grumbled response. "I'm the one with coffee in my hand."

She had a sense that he hit the day with his normal, rather cheerful demeanor, like she'd already witnessed on the morning they'd run the park. She'd thought it enticing a few days ago. Now she just felt a bit mean-spirited and more than a little gobsmacked.

Especially since he looked as good this morning as he did last night.

Better, if she were honest. The night's growth of beard over his jaw was doing funny things to her stomach and wildly enticing things to parts lower.

When he said nothing further and Marlowe couldn't be entirely sure she wasn't going to blurt out something stupid like why hadn't he come to bed with her the night before, she turned on a heel and headed for her kitchen.

And was so wrapped up in her own frustration and focus on pouring a cup of coffee that she missed the sound of his footsteps and only realized he was standing behind her when she felt the hot, enticing heat of his body against her back.

"Are you always so grumpy in the morning?"

Hardly sweet nothings or pillow talk, but the low purr of his voice against her ear—even though he hadn't touched her with his hands—was enough to have her coffee sloshing in the cup. Wyatt reached out around her and steadied the mug, his fingers covering the back of her hand. "Easy."

"I'm not grumpy."

"Excuse me." He deliberately ran a hand over her back as he stepped away. "I suppose the proper term is uncaffeinated, then."

"I don't think that's a word. And I just don't understand people who are excessively cheerful in the morning."

"I slept well, didn't you?"

"I slept fine." She took a sip of her coffee, willing the caffeine to kick in so that his eminently reasonable voice wouldn't scrape over her nerves. Because oh, my, did he look good. And all that glorious body heat pressed against her back as she'd poured her coffee had her imagining the way they'd kissed in her office.

Which, once again, only made her more frustrated he'd sent her off to bed last night like an overtired kid.

"Your couch is really comfortable. Those deep cushions were great and the sofa's plenty long that my legs weren't cramped."

"Well, good for you."

Even if it'd have been considerably more comfortable in my bed.

Only she didn't say that. Instead she turned and after another sip of her coffee tried valiantly to ignore her hormones and focus on the day ahead. "After I clean up I'm going over to my grandfather's. I know you said last night you wanted to go, but you don't have to. He just wants to know I'm alright."

"I am going. I'd like to stick close to you a bit longer so I'll see you over to his place and then on to your shop. I'd also like to ask him a few questions."

Although she didn't need a babysitter—and things felt a lot less dire with bright sunlight slipping through her small kitchen window—she also knew that Wyatt discussing the case with her grandfather would go a long way toward putting Pops at ease.

"He'll like that."

"I will, too. And we'll stop for bagels on the way and bring breakfast, too."

She shot him a gimlet eye. "You've got quite the plan going. How long have you been up?"

"Long enough to put on a pot of coffee and fold the blanket on the couch." He reached across the counter and grabbed the pot, refilling his mug, before refocusing on her. "I can't help but think you're mad at me this morning. Did I do something to upset you?"

"You're heavy-handed and bossy. And—" Marlowe stopped, aware the sexual frustration and tension that had ridden her since the night before was about to take on a whole new dimension. One that not-so-subtly suggested she was pining for him in some way.

"And what?"

"Nothing." She shook her head. "I need to go get ready for the day."

She set her mug on the counter and had turned away before his hand snaked out, grabbing hers. He pulled her close, his other arm wrapping around her. "You're not mad because we haven't kissed this morning?"

His chest was hard as it met hers—deliciously so— and warm through the material of her T-shirt. "Of course not."

Wyatt bent his head, his lips finding the edge of her jaw, just below her ear. "Because I could make it up to you. You know, if that was the problem."

Marlowe tilted her head slightly as his lips grazed the sensitive area below her ear, his breath warm against her skin while the vibrations of his voice sent shivers down her spine.

She fought to keep her annoyance in place, a ready defense against this aching need that seemed to sweep through her whenever he was around.

Because whatever this was, she didn't care for the slightly out-of-control sensation that hovered inside her, like moving a bit too quickly down a ski slope.

She didn't like to be out of control. In fact, she'd carefully ordered her life to avoid that state in every way. And yet, with Wyatt...

It all left a sort of breathless rush that was increasingly becoming addictive.

"That's not the problem."

"Okay."

The deep, husky quality of his tone vanished on that lone word as he stood up straight and backed away from her.

The change was so abrupt she scrambled for the counter, trying to catch her balance.

The mischief she saw sparking in those sky-blue eyes revealed just how well she'd been played. With a swift swat on his big, rounded shoulder, she stepped back. "You're an ass."

"And you're far too adorable in the morning."

Before she could even come up with any sort of re-action to that, he had her in his arms again, his mouth coming down to hers. Just before their lips met, he whispered, "I want you, too, Marlowe."

And then there were no words or emotions or any-thing other than sheer, liquid fire flooding her veins as his mouth consumed hers.

With bold strokes of his tongue against hers, Mar-lowe melted in Wyatt's arms, passion flaring between them like a flash fire. The restless frustration that had been a constant companion since she woke up faded at the knowledge he wasn't unaffected.

Not at all, she reminded herself as his obvious, insis-tent erection pressed seductively against her. That clear sign of his desire only pushed her own higher, her plans for the day fading away as this man quickly became the sole focus of her world.

Wyatt Trumball was all she wanted.

And, in a sudden rush of awareness she wasn't quite sure what to do with, she was fast coming to understand he might be all she needed, too.

Chapter 11

Wyatt hadn't been a teenager in nearly a decade and a half, yet sitting in Anderson McCoy's living room, spreading cream cheese on his still-warm bagel, he couldn't quite hide the flashes of embarrassed heat that kept rearing up each time he looked at Marlowe.

He was a grown man and he hadn't made excuses or snuck around with a woman since, well…what felt like forever.

But arriving at Anderson's with the man's grand-daughter in tow had struck some sort of long-dormant, almost recalcitrant emotion inside him that smacked of fifteen-year-old reactions.

Especially since it had taken everything in him to pull away from Marlowe in her kitchen this morning and suggest she go get ready to set her grandfather's mind at ease and fill him on the details from the night before.

"And there weren't any drugs this time? And, thankfully, no body," Anderson added, almost as an afterthought.

"No, sir," Wyatt said, grateful for the older man's laser focus on the topic at hand. "This safe breaks pattern."

"Which means it's escalating in a new direction."

"Even without a murder, Pops?" Marlowe took a sip of her coffee, her bagel still untouched on the table. "I thought escalation always resulted in something worse."

"It usually does, but this change in pattern could be gearing up for worse."

"Captain Reed called it a game."

"Oh, it is that," the wily old detective quickly agreed. "It's got every mark of taunting the cops. The random acts. The small cache of drugs with the bodies. And dropping a safe at the base of the bridge? That was no accident."

All of which had bothered Wyatt since he and Gav found the safe on the bridge check. The waters around New York's access points were heavily patrolled. Whoever was doing this was able to get down there to hide the safe with deliberate actions. Only a qualified diver could make the difficult trek under water and had to start that trek out of sight of the cops in the first place.

"That's it," Wyatt said, pissed it had taken him this long to realize it. "We need to look at divers. At who would possibly be qualified to do this."

"I realize your skills aren't common, but it's not impossible to find a diver, is it?"

Wyatt shook his head. "This isn't easy work in those waters. It's dark and murky and you have to have some real incentive to go down there. My money's on a disillusioned mercenary with some military training or a scuba teacher who found a way to make some cash on the side."

Anderson tapped the side of his own mug of coffee. "That's good, Wyatt. And it fits. You need talent to do that. And with talent usually comes a recognition of how to make some money off the skill."

Wyatt considered everything and realized it made sense. They'd been so focused up to now on the kayakers in the water that he'd clearly overlooked the scuba expertise needed on the last dive.

"Seems like I owe you once again, sir. I'd like to think I'd've come around to this eventually, but this is great insight."

"You would have come around to it and damn quick," Anderson said with a smile. "But it's fun for me to help. And sometimes it's just good to play theories off of someone else. Getting too deep in a case can often give tunnel vision."

Anderson shot Marlowe a pointed look.

"And it's a nice distraction from the fact my granddaughter dodged bullets last night."

"Come on, Pops. I called you."

"I know you did, Lowe. It doesn't change the fact that it happened."

She reached over and laid a hand on his. "No, I suppose it doesn't."

Anderson got a few more admonitions in as they

all shifted their focus to breakfast, but his interest had clearly been piqued by all that was going on.

"You got any leads yet on the shooter?"

"I called into the responding precinct this morning. Spoke to the lieutenant who owns the case. Nothing's popped yet but we're working on the theory it is tied to the safes, while not shutting down any other avenues of inquiry."

"Details on the safes are that widely known?" Anderson asked.

"That's the problem," Wyatt said, once again battling the subtle embarrassment he needed help and the ready gratitude Anderson was willing to share his time. "Very few details have been released. The press picked up on the kayaker story quickly, but we managed to keep the aspects of the safe out of the details. It's always possible someone rather enterprising has continued to dig, but the press office would have given me a heads-up if they caught a hit on the story."

"I know we're tying it all together," Marlowe said, tapping the side of her mug, "but could it have been a lone shooter, coincidentally acting out of some misguided anger?"

"What do I always say about coincidences, Lowe?"

Marlowe smiled at her grandfather before giving Wyatt an even wider grin. "The same thing Wyatt says. They're highly unlikely in police work. It still doesn't mean it's impossible."

"Which is why the midtown precinct who answered the call last night is running down any disgruntled employees who could have had access to that floor or known the layout well enough to wait for an opening."

Wyatt appreciated Marlowe's desire to keep an open mind but was firmly in the same camp as Anderson.

There just weren't coincidences in police work.

But why shoot at him?

Taking aim at a cop under any circumstance was a bad idea. But as a direct hit attempting to take one out? The motive didn't play for him. Those safes were all planted so they'd be discovered. Add on taking potshots at cops and you had a set of behavior that was calculated and slightly unstable.

"Are you able to share what you found in the safe, Wyatt?"

For most he'd have declined to answer, but Anderson's experience and connection to the precinct put him in a different category. Add on he and Captain Reed had remained close friends and Wyatt wasn't concerned with sharing what he knew.

"That's what's odd. The first three were all strapped to the dead kayakers and all held the kilos of heroin. This one was sunk in a place it was sure to be found and held four pieces of paper."

"That's it?"

"Three photocopies and a name scrawled with magic marker on the fourth."

Wyatt shared the specifics on the photocopied information before sharing the last piece.

"Nightwatch 1995."

Anderson's rheumy yet alert gaze went rock hard at that name before he seemed to think better of it. With a quick dart of his eyes to his granddaughter, he stood and crossed the room to pour himself another cup of coffee.

Wyatt wasn't sure what to make of the abrupt shift or

the fact that he saw the man's hand tremble as he poured the coffee.

But he knew, without question, that the man's next words were a lie.

"Sounds like someone's giving you the runaround, Wyatt. Trying to get you off the real work to play a bunch of games."

Marlowe saw the sudden change in her grandfather, her stomach nosediving in a freefall. Whatever concerns she'd held about her father's known associates and that old nightclub photo, she knew, with absolute certainty, that there was a connection to Wyatt's case.

A connection her grandfather was, unquestionably, well-aware of.

No coincidences.

There never were, she thought as an odd hopelessness filled her chest.

This was her grandfather, the most honest person she knew. Hell, she considered herself a pretty honest person, as well. Yet one small link to her father and she'd betrayed every single thing she believed about herself and the way she chose to live as an adult.

More, she'd hidden it from Wyatt. Whatever was between them was new, developing, but not sharing the grainy internet photo with him had been a clear act of self-preservation.

One that now seemed particularly stark in the cold light of morning and her grandfather's shift in behavior.

Behavior he clearly had a handle on when he turned back from the counter. "Dwayne really does have the right idea. Games to draw you off the scent is what this sounds like. Your time's better spent running down a diver with the right skills."

"I can juggle a few angles here. The whole team can."

That congenial, respectful tone never wavered, but Marlowe didn't miss the subtle wariness that filled Wyatt's gaze. Or the distinct hardness that glittered in his blue gaze.

"Sure, sure," her grandfather quickly agreed. "All reminds me of a case years ago. Went down in the heart of Sunset Bay and the catacombs."

"Catacombs, Pops?" Marlowe asked. The change in subject was a bit odd, but her grandfather's reference was one she'd never heard before.

"The smugglers' tunnels along the water. They've been abandoned for years, mostly just popular with graffiti artists who try to resurrect the space every decade or so until the problem gets to be too much and they get rousted out."

"I thought the city took care of those tunnels years ago," Wyatt asked. "Sealed them all up. We don't even do dive detail on them."

Anderson shrugged. "City does close them and then some enterprising folks figure out a way to open them up again."

Wyatt's narrowed gaze was thoughtful. "You say this situation with the safes is like a case down there?"

"A lot like it. That feeling it's all a big game pervaded that case, too."

The tenor of the conversation might have shifted, but Marlowe wasn't following why anyone would even take the time to play games. She wasn't an expert on the criminal mind, but she'd always sort of assumed those trying to stay off the radar didn't go out of their way to attract attention.

Wouldn't taunting the cops be the opposite of that?

"I'm not questioning your collective instincts, but it feels like a waste of time and a hell of a lot of risk. Why do that?"

"It's not a waste of time if you think it'll divert attention off the real crime," Wyatt said.

His point had her grandfather nodding. "It was back in the mid-eighties. A local gang figured out a way to use the tunnels. Made them home turf for quite a few months before someone got a tip more was going on in there than some artists or kids messing around to get high."

"How'd they get caught?"

"Got lazy. Thought they were fooling the cops by planting evidence around the city, always drawing attention away from the water."

"But the cops figured it out," Marlowe said. "And they did it before every storefront and intersection had a security camera."

"They did, Lowe. Criminals don't do the best job of keeping their mouths shut. And too many gangs are willing to talk when an avenue's shut down to them but wide open to others. A few other gangs caught wind of how convenient those tunnels would be to hide their own work. Then got seriously pissed when they couldn't get access."

"No honor among thieves," Marlowe murmured, thinking of her father's work. He'd made it a long time without getting caught. Although he rarely spoke to her about his work, it was a fact he'd let slip once. Claimed that working alone had been the secret to his success.

Oddly, it had been her own personal mantra in her line of work. Only instead of risking the encroachment of other thugs, she only had to worry about people getting too close.

Wasn't that what she'd done with Wyatt?

She kept people at a distance and she liked it that way.

Yet here she was, interested in Wyatt—way down deep interested—and already battling what she would and would not say to him.

It was an odd reinforcement of why she liked being alone.

The thought continued to linger as her grandfather went into a rambling story about how they eventually caught the gang and got the tunnels sealed up again, but Marlowe couldn't deny how the discussion had shifted.

What had started as a genuine sharing of information now felt stilted. And, oddly, she admitted, like dinner with her mother the night before. She'd spent the entire evening convinced all of them were speaking parts, but never really taking the conversation a level deeper.

Or saying what was fundamentally the truth.

Why did she feel like that now?

And why was she suddenly so convinced Pops was hiding something very, very big?

Wyatt stared down at the waters of the Hudson River and allowed the morning to play through his mind. He and Gavin were working with the FDNY this afternoon to dive through a damaged boat that was at the core of an arson investigation and they were waiting on some details before they began.

They were on point for the evidence recovery and then after everything was cleared a salvage crew would bring up the small pleasure boat from where it had settled just south of the George Washington Bridge.

"Did you know there were smugglers tunnels in Sunset Bay?"

Gavin looked up from where he checked the gauges on his tank. "The ones along the shore, south of the shopping district?" When Wyatt only nodded, Gavin added, "They covered them in our training, but I thought they'd been closed so long they'd almost become like one of those city legends. More of a fun old story than anything with substance."

"Apparently they had quite a bit of substance for a while. Talked to Anderson McCoy this morning. He said they were the center of an investigation in the eighties. A particularly enterprising gang had used them for a solid six months, improving their business quite a bit with their little shoreline hidey holes."

"Why'd Anderson bring it up? You think there's still something going on in the tunnels? Now?"

Wyatt wasn't sure of anything, which was the reason he brought it up to Gavin at all. He trusted the man implicitly, but he also wanted someone to bounce it all off of.

"That's what doesn't play. Anderson mentioned it, relative to the recovery of the safes."

Interest clearly piqued, Gavin probed on that. "How so?"

Wyatt relayed the earlier discussion and that continued suggestion there was some sort of game afoot with whoever was masterminding the safes. How Anderson had used the gang crimes in the eighties as another example when the NYPD was run in circles by a group of thugs.

Wyatt did stop short of mentioning the odd signals he got off of Anderson, though. He hadn't imagined the older man's response—Wyatt didn't doubt himself in the least on front—but he wasn't ready to put suspicions in anyone's mind about the well-respected, retired cop, either.

But he would get to the bottom of it.

"Why don't we run past there after shift?" Gavin suggested. "Take a look around a bit. Anderson McCoy's knowledge of Sunset Bay is some of the best and deepest there is. The man *is* the freaking 86th. Maybe he's making a connection even if he didn't mean it that way."

"You read my mind."

"Since that's my job definition above and below the water, let's do it. I'll text Arlo to meet us there, as well, see if it sparks anything for him, either."

Gavin gave him a hard look. "We're going to get to the bottom of this, Trumball."

Wyatt nodded, a big part of him seasoned enough to know there came a stage in every large investigation that felt empty. But even when the work was a grind, there were answers.

He needed to separate that feeling from breakfast this morning with Marlowe's grandfather. Anderson had been incredibly forthcoming in each conversation he'd ever had with the man. Yet the moment Wyatt had uttered the word "Nightwatch" Anderson's entire demeanor had changed.

There was an alertness there and a distinct shift in the tone of their conversation that still bothered him, no matter how he turned it over in his mind.

But maybe Gavin was right.

The grizzled old cop might deserve his respect, but the man was still in his eighties. Maybe Anderson had made the connection between the safes and the tunnels off some old synaptic connection, even if it wasn't readily obvious in the retelling.

Because chalking it up to a simple story about cocky criminals making life miserable for the cops? The idea of law enforcement might be a relatively modern construct, but that push-pull was a tale as old as the human experience. There likely wasn't a cop on the force who couldn't tell a similar story.

Activity kicked up on the FDNY boat, pulling their attention. Wyatt waved back to the team on the deck. "Looks like they're ready for us."

They exchanged a few more instructions over the radio comms while their team member navigating the Zodiac positioned Wyatt and Gavin over the dive site and Wyatt was grateful for the sudden flurry of activity.

He and Gavin had a plan after work and that had to be enough. Right now, he needed the quiet of the water and the focus on something else while his subconscious worked through the mysteries of the safes.

He'd learned early in his career that sometimes deliberately thinking about something else provided the only way to shake loose a fresh idea.

But damn, this one had him in its hooks.

The sense an answer existed, just out of reach, nagged at him. But like movement out of the corner of his eye, Wyatt couldn't seem to catch it.

Which meant it was time to focus on something else and hope he'd get a handle on what had him so upside down later.

Marlowe?

The case?

The random gunshots the night before?

All of the above, Wyatt suspected, as he fitted in his breathing apparatus into his mouth and positioned himself at the edge of the Zodiac.

Time to stop thinking and start doing.

Falling back, the dark water encased him and silence immediately muted his world as he oriented himself in the Hudson. The water depth maxed out at about seventy feet in this part of the river and he and Gavin made the descent fairly quickly, the wreckage of the boat coming into focus where it had settled in the silty bottom.

As they neared the recreational pleasure boat they separated, each focused on their pre-agreed search areas. The starboard hull was burned out just as they'd been prepped, and he could make out the stern where it lay embedded in the river floor. He'd take care of removing whatever evidence he could get off the inboard engine while Gavin sought any gasoline or chemical residue up in the small cabin housing the steering wheel.

The working theory was the boat had been taken out and torched by an angry mistress who wasn't happy to be downgraded to an ex. The owner of the pleasure boat had reported it missing out of the 79th Street Boat Basin and cameras had caught a woman's cloaked figure approaching the marina the night before.

Although he didn't condone the crime, Wyatt had to give the woman props for an impressive revenge plot. Not only did it take a lot of anger to do this level of damage, but the working theory was she'd done it all on her own, which was both careless and shockingly determined.

Wyatt used various tools to pry open the panel that housed the engine, working carefully to keep as clean a sample as he could. Although the woman was a primary suspect and the damage was consistent with arson, they had to rule out innocence, as well. His retrieval of the engine—presumably one without any signs of distress or wear that would put this firmly in the realm of accident—was essential. He knew his job and worked carefully to preserve the sample.

He nearly had the engine loose, the murky water and angle of the boat where it had settled in the riverbed making the work slow-going, when Wyatt felt the distinct sense of movement behind him.

Animal?

Debris?

A shot of awareness spiked hard as he realized that sense had become a distinct form, suddenly locked on him, with the build and motion and strength of a human. Wyatt just made out the solid figure of another diver when a hard tug pulled on his tank. The thick form wrapped around him with shocking speed, pressing him tight against the side of the boat. The other diver used Wyatt's splayed position against the undamaged portion of the hull for the engine retrieval to his advantage, pinning him in place.

He tried to struggle, moving on pure instinct to strike back, but the other diver was like an octopus, his arms and legs moving in a strange synchronicity that ensured he'd had time to plan this assault.

Forcing a calm he didn't feel in order to control his breathing, Wyatt lifted his hand in an uppercut, aiming for the guy's breathing apparatus or mask—whatever he could get a clean shot at—when a distinct change filled his own mask.

But those octopus moves had been deliberate and Wyatt recognized it immediately as he saw his breathing apparatus separate, the low pressure tube that connected to his tank floating in the murky water where it had been cut clean through.

The abrupt release of pressure against his body jarred Wyatt as panic, sudden and absolute, gripped him in tight fists. The other guy was already moving away as Wyatt reached for his bailout bottle, only to understand what that initial tug on his tanks was all about.

The bastard had his bailout bottle, too.

Which meant Wyatt was seventy feet below the surface with no way up.

He fought to keep that panic at bay, slamming a hand on the boat to get Gavin's attention. Banging on the hull wherever he could find an undamaged place to beat his fist, he moved steadily toward his partner, aware the need to share air was a more pressing concern than risking a trip to the surface.

Even as each second passed without any fresh air hitting his lungs.

The burned sections of the hull felt endless as Wyatt moved diligently toward Gavin. As he reached the portion of the boat that held the cabin he could see Gavin moving inside, oblivious to the distress. Banging on the walls, the hull, and then finally grabbing his partner's foot, Wyatt desperately aimed for a calm he didn't feel.

He needed his focus.

And he needed Gavin.

Gav turned immediately at Wyatt's firm hold on his foot, his eyes going wide behind his mask as Wyatt laid a hand over his throat and then pointed at his breathing apparatus.

Whatever else they'd been taught, to focus on your partner first was priority.

Always.

Gavin moved out of the cabin immediately, his attention on Wyatt. Without hesitation, he removed his breather and handed it over and Wyatt concentrated on taking a solid, measured breath instead of the gulp his panicked instincts demanded.

His partner watched him through it, his gaze never leaving Wyatt's as those deep, steady breaths filled his chest.

On a nod, Wyatt handed the breather over, sharing the air with his partner. He gave Gavin time to breathe several breaths of his own before he took the breather again. Once he handed it back, they moved out of the cabin and swam away from the boat, their gazes scanning the cloudy water around them.

Assured they didn't see anyone lying in wait, they continued their movements in unison, an unbreakable unit. And with steady, constant movements began the ascent to the surface.

Chapter 12

"What in the ever-loving hell was that?"

Gavin had repeated that phrase, along with several colorful curses Wyatt would have admired under better circumstances, over and over. His partner had moved from shock to seething anger and back to shock for the past twenty minutes.

And all Wyatt could do was stare at his hands and replay what had happened under the water.

Where had the bastard come from?

Even as he knew the real question—the far more important one—was why? Why had he come after a set of highly trained NYPD divers in the midst of a shift?

What was the endgame?

Whatever Wyatt had believed up to now—and he was already damn sure there was something big going on—the discovery of those safes had to be at the heart of everything.

And somehow, some way, he'd become the face of the case.

The real question was if he was some sort of collateral damage to a bigger prize, or if this was all directed at him.

Because he'd discovered the first safe?

Because he was a target from something he'd worked on earlier in his career?

Or again, Wyatt thought in disgust, just that collateral damage in service to some bigger outcome.

The dispatch team had sent another set of divers out to the site to finish the retrieval he and Gavin had started, with the express instruction neither he nor Gav could go down on another dive today.

He'd never been that spooked by his job—and he'd had instances in the past that had certainly tested the limits of his personal fortitude—but this was a whole other ball game. Add on the mandatory shot of antibiotics he and Gav had already been administered for their oral exposure to the waters of the Hudson, and he'd chalk it up to a grand sort of day.

Dispatch had also sent a team to patrol the waters for the diver to surface, but Wyatt already knew they wouldn't find anything.

That guy was long gone.

Because whatever else he was, he had experience, training and a damn fine set of skills beneath the water. A set of skills that Wyatt had revised in his mind to both mercenary and ex-military since there was no way to build a set of capabilities like that without serious training.

He had the scuba experience, the muscle and the ability to take out a trained enemy.

He was going to counsel Dwayne to bring in some federal assistance if possible to start looking into someone who fit that profile. This person might have a disgruntled reputation layered on top of a government-funded background in lethal combat and recognizance tactics.

And as Wyatt considered it all, he knew something dark was going on.

While miniscule in the realm of the broader drug trade, the kilos of heroin in the first three safes still had street value.

Hits on cops required a sizable cash payment.

And scuba skills like he'd just dealt with?

Just more proof that nothing about this whole operation was cheap or easy.

Captain Reed was waiting for him and Gav on the dock as they came back into Sunset Bay. Since his equipment needed to be moved into evidence, Wyatt had turned to do that first, unwilling to let his tools out of his sight.

But Dwayne anticipated the move and boarded the boat, coming into the wheelhouse.

"Trumball? How are you doing?"

Since he was still fighting a round of shivers that seemed determined to turn the afternoon into a total loss, Wyatt kept his hands at his side and shot Dwayne a smile he was pretty sure missed cocky by a mile. "I'll live."

"I suppose you will, but that wasn't my question."

Dwayne's dark skin creased in tense lines before he sighed, gesturing Wyatt toward a small table they used to lay out maps and plan a dive. "Sit down with me a bit."

Wyatt took the seat as instructed.

"Walk me through it."

His captain might have been briefed already, but Dwayne Reed had that incredibly special ability to actually listen. He gave his full attention to the conversation, only asking a few clarifying questions until Wyatt got through it all.

"You had no sense the man was there?"

"Not a bit. Gavin and I were focused on the work, but one minute I'm trying to dig out the engine and preserve the evidence and the next the bastard was on me."

Wyatt had been over and over it in his mind and no matter how he considered it, he had no idea how he could have played it differently. He wanted to believe his instincts could have been sharper or his sense of someone approaching keener, but how the hell did you suss out a silent threat in the murky waters of the Hudson River?

Especially when there shouldn't have been a human threat in those waters in the first place.

Unbidden, his own memories of the dive had twisted up with how he imagined his father's last trip beneath the water.

Through the years his study of his father's last dive had consumed him. He'd been over and over it in his mind's eye, imagining it all. And no matter what his father had dealt with—no matter how terrible the panic at the end—that dive had still been a result of a horrible disaster.

A risk—freely taken—that had resulted in tragedy. But this afternoon?

Wyatt had avoided an attempted murder, plain and simple.

"Sounds like we've been looking at this all wrong."

"How so, sir?"

"We've been thinking of those safes as a diversion or a game to distract us."

"You think it's something else?"

"I absolutely do." Dwayne's mouth set in a grim, hard line as his dark eyes darted to Wyatt's destroyed equipment, piled near the door to the wheelhouse. "I have no doubt in my mind, in fact."

"About what?"

"Those safes are bait, pure and simple."

Marlowe raced through the Brooklyn neighborhood she'd called home for the past decade and abstractly noticed the early evening air had a slight chill to it. Summer was giving way to fall and while she normally loved that feeling, all she could do was put one foot in front of the other as fast as possible.

Her sole focus was getting to Wyatt.

She ran along the western side of the park, weaving her way toward the apartment Arlo had told her was Wyatt's.

Marlowe had no idea when her favored nation status as Anderson McCoy's granddaughter had flipped over to full cred on her own, but she was wildly grateful that the detective had called her and given her a heads-up on what happened to Wyatt earlier that day.

As well as trusting her with Wyatt's address.

She turned the last block and raced up the steps of the stoop on the brownstone that Arlo had noted as Wyatt's, taking them two at a time. Worry churned her stomach and she shifted from foot to foot as she waited for him to answer his apartment bell.

Was he okay?

Arlo claimed he was but had remained tightlipped about the rest of what had happened. Only that Wyatt had been in a scary situation earlier that day and she should give him a call.

"Hello?"

Wyatt's voice came through the speaker, strong and true, and Marlowe felt the first notch of tension slip. "It's me, Marlowe."

The buzzer rang before she could say anything more and she pushed into the foyer of the brownstone, glancing at the row of stairs in front of her. Before she could start up, a door opened on the first floor, Wyatt in the entry.

Whatever fear had carried her this far pushed her forward, straight into his arms. "Are you okay?"

He pulled her close, his arms tight around her, his lips pressed to the side of her head. "I'm good."

She heard the quaver in his voice and felt the light tremors that shuddered through his body.

Was he okay?

Keeping her hold tight, she pulled back to look up at him. "Arlo called and—"

The words vanished as his mouth took hers, the

fervor of his kiss something she met immediately, allowing the passion and need between them to simply consume her.

Something raw and wanting and more than a little desperate flared between them and she marveled at the thick drumbeat of desire that had a drugging sort of excitement flooding her veins.

What was this they shared?

Why had she fought it for so long?

And why—

Once again, her ability to string thoughts together vanished as her whole world shrank down to that moment with Wyatt.

His tongue melded with hers, an erotic welcome that held as much promise as need. That shudder she'd felt as her arms had wrapped around him faded a bit, replaced with a physical intensity that spoke as much of need as it did a yearning to hold on to something real.

Solid.

Alive.

Marlowe couldn't deny him any of it, even as she still wondered exactly what had happened. Arlo's details had remained deliberately vague—his insistence that it was Wyatt's story to tell—but she knew it was bad. Had gotten that clearly from what Arlo didn't say in addition to the dark undertone beneath his words.

And still, despite wanting answers, she couldn't stop touching him.

Long moments later she heard the slam of the front door of the brownstone and realized they still stood in the open entryway to Wyatt's apartment. She pulled back as he shot a wink at the woman who stood near the stairwell, two cloth bags of groceries hanging by her sides.

"Hi, Wyatt."

"Hey, Zoe."

"You putting on a show for the super?" She lifted a hand in the direction of the ceiling. "Those hallway cameras are catching an eyeful."

A heavy blush worked its way up her neck as Marlowe shifted in Wyatt's arms, trying to face his neighbor to introduce herself. Since Wyatt still had a firm hold on her it was hard to do that with any measure of dignity so Marlowe finally gave up and smiled over her shoulder. "Hey, there. I'm Marlowe."

"The lock lady." Zoe shot her a broad smile. "Nice to meet you. I'm Zoe."

Marlowe wasn't sure if she wanted to know how Zoe knew of her so she just gave a small wave back. "That's me."

"Yo, Wyatt. My grandmother said you had a hard day. You doing okay?"

"I'm good." Wyatt's gaze dropped to Marlowe's before winging back to his cute neighbor. "Better now."

"I'll just leave you to it, then. You two have a good night. I'm off to make some art. After, of course, I enjoy the strawberry ice cream that's currently melting in one of these bags."

Zoe was off up the main stairwell of the brownstone as fast as she'd arrived and it left Marlowe in that awkward hold where she and Wyatt sort of still clung to each other. "Um. She's nice."

"Z's great. She's lived here about a year. She's an

artist and since she was raised in the neighborhood she somehow knows everyone."

"That's how she knows what happened to you?"

"The neighborhood takes care of their own."

A vague reminder that something big had happened. With that thought, Marlowe finally found a way to disengage herself from his hold, but not before pressing a quick kiss to his jaw. "Invite me in and tell me about what happened. Arlo was insistent I call you but vague on the details."

In the request, Marlowe saw the vulnerability. It was brief, flashing quickly before he tamped it down, but it was clearly there. And in that moment, she realized that the man who'd just demolished every last inhibition she possessed was struggling with a very large problem.

She'd always see Wyatt as a larger-than-life figure. Even when their interactions were more steeped in his teasing and her responding eye rolls, she'd known him for his solid strength and capable demeanor.

Yet here.

Now.

He was badly shaken.

Willing the stormy, fiery passion that always flared between them to the back burner, she reached for his hand and tugged him forward, closing the door with her other hand.

Once they were inside his apartment, all alone, she turned to Wyatt, her voice soft. "Tell me."

Marlowe still struggled to process the whole story ten minutes later where she sat opposite Wyatt on the couch.

Attempted murder?

Under water and while doing his job?

"Are you sure you're okay?"

"I'm better now that you're here." He extended a hand and laid it over hers. "That's not a line, Marlowe. I'm glad you're here and I can honestly say I'm more settled than I have been since it happened. I just—"

He broke off, scrubbing a hand over the back of his head before standing to pace. "I just keep going over and over it. How the bastard got the jump on us. How he knew where we'd be. How—" Something bleak settled in that blue gaze, turning it to ice.

"How he possibly did this. We're not an amateur operation, despite what this looks like."

"Of course you're not. You're highly trained professionals and the NYPD is one of the most sophisticated police operations in the world."

Her support seemed to add to his fire, his voice rising as he kept pacing. "We have process and protocol. We have patrols. People don't just go swimming in the waters around New York, shooting kayakers, dropping safes against bridges and attacking NYPD officers. It's just surreal."

"He's a professional, Wyatt. A determined one at that."

"But what's his bigger goal? What the hell is this all about?"

Marlowe wished she knew, but she also knew that she owed him her honesty about her father.

About the known associates she'd discovered in that old photo online.

Wyatt nearly lost his life today and no matter the risk

to her father's parole, he needed every detail he could get his hands on to understand what was going on. It wasn't just a matter of putting away a criminal. It had become a matter of life and death.

"I need to talk to you about something."

His gaze sharpened once more, that quick reminder that whatever else he was, Wyatt was a cop.

"What is it?"

"It's about my father."

If he was surprised by her shift in topic, he didn't show it, instead taking the seat next to her again. "I know that's a tough topic for you. I've avoided asking you about him but I know the back story there." He looked uncomfortable but pressed on. "Most everyone at the 86th does. They don't gossip about it out of respect for your grandfather, but people do know about your father's crimes."

Marlowe had suspected as much, but it was some comfort to know that underlying and everlasting respect for Pops kept the story of her father in perspective for others.

"Unlike my mother's approach of trying to lie it away, it's just an aspect of my life I avoid talking about. I've moved past it and made a life for myself. Wallowing in the reality of who he is hasn't ever done much for my mental health and I learned a long time ago to set it aside."

"That doesn't mean it doesn't affect you. He is your father, Marlowe."

"No, it doesn't. And it's a lesson I've come to realize, with stark clarity, this week."

When Wyatt didn't say anything in response, nor did he press her, Marlowe realized it was all on her.

And, she had to admit, it was time.

Time to tell him the truth. Her own and the underlying truth about the father she loved, even as she'd had to mentally cut him out of her life in order to have a life.

"There are very few doors, locked or otherwise, my father has ever had any trouble getting through."

"Because he's a thief?"

"Because he's a charming thief." She shook her head, thinking even now about the man who still had a solid amount of sparkle and shine, even clad head to toe in prison orange. "And it draws people to him, believing in him even when there's a sleight of hand taking place behind his back."

"Like your mother?"

"I think my mother is the best example, but it wasn't just her. Everyone in Michael McCoy's orbit spends far longer there than they should because they're enjoying themselves so damn much."

She considered her grandfather, the most upstanding and honest person she knew. "It killed my grandfather. Slowly, over time, but I truly believe if my father hadn't finally been caught for his crimes it would have been the death of my grandfather."

"How so?"

"The disappointment. It's so deep and so severe. His son chose a life in direct opposition to all he believes in."

"Has he talked to you about it?"

She smiled at that, the limited conversations she and Pops had spoken over the years consisting of minimally voiced statements, only when pressed by outside circumstances like a parole hearing or an outreach by Michael's lawyer that needed handling.

"Like me, my grandfather's a vault. So that's more what I've pieced together than anything he and I have really discussed."

"Is that healthy?"

"Maybe yes, maybe no. But it is a rhythm we've managed to find over the years. Because there's processing grief and then there's a day when you decide that it can't be the dominant force in your life any longer. Pops and I have both done that. Or I thought we had until this past week."

"Is this about your grandfather's weird response this morning to our conversation?"

"Yes, but it's about me, too."

"What's really going on, Marlowe?"

"I don't know if I'm right or not, but I think I might have found a connection to your case."

"To the safes?"

"To the weird papers inside the last safe. And that scrawled name. Nightwatch."

"What do you know?"

"I found a dated photo online. Some men standing in front of an old nightclub in Brooklyn called Nightwatch. One of the men was noted in files as one of my father's known associates."

Wyatt's face was like granite, his jaw set in a line so hard she was surprised he didn't crack teeth.

Rushing on, she tried her best to explain herself, even as she suspected there wasn't much she could say to sway him.

And still, she had to try.

"I didn't mention it because I wanted to look into it on my own. I wanted to talk to my father and give him a chance to explain. To tell me more."

"You wanted to talk to him? This man you claim you've cut out of your life? You wanted to talk to him instead of bringing it to me, in the midst of an active investigation."

"I needed to know more, Wyatt. That's all and then I was going to tell you."

"You've known this? For a while?"

"When you came to my office yesterday afternoon I'd just found it online." She knew how it looked, but she had every intention of telling him. After she'd had a better idea of what she'd seen. "I swear, I wasn't going to hold this back, I just—"

"You just what? Thought it was okay to hold back information in an active police investigation?"

"No, I—"

"I, I, I! This isn't about you, Marlowe!" Wyatt stood again, his features a mix of anger and a raw sort of disappointment that lasered straight to the center of her chest. "I let you in on this. I trusted you. I trusted that you know enough about how police work was managed that you could act responsibly with the information you were privy to."

"But I did! I saw one old photo online. That's all. My father has a right to answer a few questions before he's somehow implicated in what's going on. That's all I wanted. To ask a few questions before making connections that might mean nothing. I couldn't risk him losing his parole over something that might be a coincidence."

A hard laugh spilled from Wyatt's lips. "Right. Because we've only talked at length that there are no coincidences."

"But maybe it is. Maybe—"

She broke off as Wyatt's eyes went wide.

"What?" Marlowe asked, aware the man she'd kissed in the doorway and attempted to comfort had completely vanished.

In its place was a hard-edged cop without an ounce of concern for her father's future.

"That's what this morning was about."

"What do you mean? What about this morning?"

"Anderson." Wyatt shook his head. "He knows something, too."

"What could he possibly know? No one knows anything right now. That's why I need to talk to my father."

"No." Wyatt shook his head. But it was his low, murmured words that had Marlowe's heart breaking.

Not because she thought he was wrong.

But because she was deadly afraid he was right.

"Your grandfather knew something the moment I uttered the word Nightwatch."

Chapter 13

Wyatt stared at his computer screen, his eyes blurring at the overload of blue light.

And exhaustion.

And such a bone-deep disappointment he wasn't sure what to do with it.

How could Marlowe keep that news from him? She'd discovered a clear connection to his case—one she'd pulled up for him on his home computer before he drove her home.

The drive had been awkward and in direct opposition to the greeting they'd shared when she'd arrived. Where their conversation up to now had flowed freely, the silence between had been stilted and staid. And even as a small, sneaking sense of guilt had settled into his gut over his actions, he couldn't change it.

And, damn it, he had a right to be pissed off.

For a man Marlowe claimed she'd cut from her life, her willingness to trust her father before him chaffed.

Hell, it rubbed him raw.

Sitting here at his desk, poring over old files at one in the morning, wasn't making it any better.

He'd given Arlo a heads-up and whatever he found he'd pass on so his fellow detective could pick up the ball the next morning. But now that he'd also found out he and Gav were sitting out dives for the next three days, there wasn't any reason he couldn't take care of the extra legwork for Arlo.

It would at least give him something productive and active to do.

Something that might take his mind off Marlowe.

"Trumball, what are you still doing here? Especially after the day you had."

Wyatt looked up to find Captain Reed standing on the other side of his desk.

"I could ask you the same. And I'm still here especially because of the day I had."

Their bullpen arrangement of the detectives' work area meant Wyatt only had a lone chair that sat beside his desk, but Dwayne sank into it easily. "Hell of a day all around."

"Why are you still here?" Wyatt asked. Dwayne was an incredibly hardworking captain, but also a committed family man and hours like this were usually tied to a very specific case.

"Homicide got a big one in late this afternoon. By the time he lawyered up and the team took a shot at him, successfully, I might add, it was just shy of midnight."

Wyatt had heard some word of what was going on

when he'd arrived back at the precinct after dropping Marlowe off, but hadn't realized the interrogation had run that late. "And you're still here because?"

"Because I'm still keyed up and thought I'd work for a bit." Dwayne flashed a bright white smile. "I can't say I've been all that successful notching the adrenaline back down."

"Some days are like that."

"What are you working on?"

Wyatt wasn't going to hold a damn thing back from his captain, but he didn't want to implicate Marlowe negatively, either. And certainly not Anderson until he had a full sense of what they were dealing with.

So instead, he opted for as simple an answer as possible and hoped like hell he wasn't committing the same lie by omission Marlowe had.

"Marlowe McCoy's father is about to come up for his parole hearing. In the process of looking through some paperwork from her father's lawyer, she came across some details on his last case. She got curious and did some internet diving."

Dwayne was clearly interested, his dark eyes sharp. Focused. "She find something we couldn't?"

"She did, sir."

Without any further preamble, Wyatt turned his computer screen toward Dwayne, the image of Michael McCoy's known associates standing in front of the Night-watch club filling the space.

"Son of a bitch." The exhale was hard and Dwayne added a few more curses for good measure. "I don't believe it."

"I didn't at first, either, but it's a clear connection."

"And what we've been searching for."

"It's a start but the rest is still as puzzling as ever."

Wyatt hadn't had any luck on the other photocopied sheets from the safe.

He'd done several searches on the jewel exhibit that had been featured in the photocopied *New York Times* article. All that had come up was that a display of jewels had been on loan for three months, with the centerpiece of the exhibit a legendary Burmese ruby. He'd exhausted the NYPD archives and found nothing of substance on the exhibit other than a handful of vice bookings that had happened on the streets around the museum and a few assault and batteries that had been filed during that time, as well.

The event went off, seemingly, without a hitch.

The photocopied parking ticket had been a lost cause from the start. Even if he had been able to lift a license plate number off the ticket, their entire system had been archived in the late nineties and they'd have had to go digging in the NYPD archives to find the details.

Wyatt would have done it, too—he hated the archives warehouse but he wasn't a stranger to it when he needed information—but the lack of plate numbers made the photocopy useless.

And then the last piece—a diner receipt in Brooklyn—was the most puzzling.

Whoever put the packet of papers together did it with some intent. But all he came back to each time was lingering feelings of being toyed with.

Taunted, really.

"None of it makes sense, Dwayne."

His captain tapped the edge of his desk with his index

finger. "It's been a long day all the way around. Maybe it's time to give it a rest tonight."

"Yeah."

Dwayne nodded. "I know you and Gav are off the dive schedule for a few days, but let's do a briefing tomorrow afternoon. I want us to get a handle on every possible way that guy got underneath the water and to you."

"He's a professional. And the water's muddy enough if he knew how to stay low no one would have spotted him."

"More reason we need to get on top of this and get it figured out. I put a call into a buddy of mine at the Bureau. Skills like that suggest ex-military, like we've been saying."

Wyatt was surprised by the decision. "You know if you bring them in with something that specific they're going to get involved."

Dwayne's smile was broad. "Why do you think I did it? Someone with federal training doing mercenary jobs against my cops? I want it figured out and I want them throwing every resource they've got on it."

"Thank you, sir. That means a lot."

His captain just stood. "I'm heading home and I suggest you do the same."

"Just going to wrap up a note to Arlo. Then I'm heading out."

"See that you do."

Wyatt watched Dwayne walk away and, not for the first time, was grateful for the family he had at the 86th. Bringing in the Feds on something like his and Gav's dive would most certainly muddy the jurisdictional waters and the Feds would likely toss their weight around a bit. Yet Dwayne hadn't hesitated.

He did right by his cops and he took the politics on himself.

It was a gift to have leadership like that. One he didn't take lightly.

Which brought him right back around to Anderson McCoy. The retired chief of detectives had a stellar reputation, even after being off the force for nearly two decades.

Was that reputation misplaced?

Before this morning's discussion in the man's kitchen, Wyatt would never have even considered it a possibility.

But now?

He was deeply concerned the man held the key to a large secret he'd rather keep buried.

Marlowe hit the main circuit around the park just as the sun rose up over the tops of the trees. A few other early morning joggers were out as well as several people walking dogs in the cool breeze.

She normally loved this time of year. The last days of summer were giving way to fall and the air had a breeziness that kept her run comfortable. The rhythm of the city changed, with kids back in school and the shorter days ultimately ceding to falling leaves and crisp nights.

But not yet, she reminded herself as she hit the mental marker for mile one.

For now she'd enjoy what was left of the last dying days of summer.

And she wouldn't think too hard on the decision she'd

made the night before as she lay tossing and turning in bed.

Those moments with Wyatt, confessing to him what she'd discovered, had been some of the worst of her adult life. His gaze—all cop—had morphed from sharp and dangerous to deeply disappointed as she'd struggled to explain her hesitance to tell him.

She wanted to talk to her father.

That was all.

It was the only reason she'd held back on showing that internet photo to Wyatt. She wanted a half hour with her father, using the time to ask him about those men and understand his connection.

No matter what her father eventually told her, she was going to tell Wyatt. She'd never have kept it from him, regardless of the answer she got from her dad.

But damn it, she'd wanted the time to actually get an answer.

Was that too much to ask?

Her father had been in jail nearly her entire adult life. She'd accepted long ago that their visits would consist of discussions through glass in the winter and the hawk-like audience of prison guards in a small courtyard in summer. It was the reality of the life he'd chosen and she had come to a place in her own life where she accepted it.

But if he had a real shot at getting out after serving his debt to society, was it so wrong she wanted to ensure he had that shot?

The man was in prison, for Pete's sake. There was no way he was actually involved in Wyatt's case. All

she'd wanted was a chance to get some information before creating questions about his innocence.

She knew what it was to have people look at you sideways, even if you hadn't done anything. Yes, she'd chosen to stay in Brooklyn, but for the people who knew her
or of her through her family's history, she would always
be Michael's daughter, potentially at risk for doing bad.

Her chosen profession likely didn't help, Marlowe
acknowledged with a small smile as she rounded the
curve for mile two, but it still wasn't fair.

Even if you did keep details from Wyatt.

That small voice taunted her from underneath the
self-righteous conviction that she had a right to talk
to her dad.

"Damn it." She let out the short curse, shocked when
a voice echoed from beside her, pulling her out of her
head.

"You're out here early."

She nearly fumbled her steps and only Wyatt's steady-
ing hand on her elbow prevented her from losing her
footing.

"Easy."

"What are you doing here?"

He dropped his hand from her arm and kept pace
next to her. "Couldn't sleep."

"And you decided to come find me?"

"I decided to take a run and hoped I'd find you."

She side-eyed him as they kept a steady pace. "After
last night, I didn't think you'd want to see me at all."

"After last night, that's the exact reason I want to
see you."

Marlowe kept running, unsure what to say. His behavior the night before was frustrating and upsetting, but she couldn't exactly blame him for his anger, either. If the situation was reversed, she'd likely have done the same.

Hadn't that been the very problem she'd struggled with, tossing and turning all night?

She wanted to be mad at Wyatt but there was a solid streak of mad at herself.

And a rock and a hard place decision she wasn't sure she'd make differently, even if she were given the chance to go back and do it again.

"Look, can we talk?"

Wyatt slowed to telegraph his intentions and Marlowe followed suit, heading for a nearby bench. They stood and stretched for a few minutes before finally taking a seat.

"First, I'm sorry for my reaction last night. I was upset and—"

Whatever she was expecting, an immediate apology wasn't it and Marlowe stopped him mid-apology. "I'm sorry, too, even though there's a big part of me that feels like it's disingenuous of me to apologize."

"Why's that?"

The early morning sun fell through a break in the trees behind him, spearing shoots of light over Wyatt. She couldn't dismiss the deep sense of exhaustion that rode him or the dark circles under his eyes.

"I really wasn't trying to deceive you, Wyatt. I wanted to give my father a chance to explain, that's all. Whatever his answer, it wouldn't have stopped me from telling you what I found."

Whatever mental gymnastics she'd gone through

over waiting to tell Wyatt about the photo, she was beyond certain of that fact.

And as he studied her in the morning light, his gaze was oddly understanding, that hard glitter of cop eyes nowhere in sight. "I think I understand."

"It's why I'm going to see him this afternoon. I want to get this over with and get my answers."

"You shouldn't pull him into this, Marlowe. It's an active investigation and he can't know the details. Prisons aren't nearly as locked down as you might think. He can't have information like this."

"I'm not going to tell him about the investigation. I want to ask him about the men who were already mentioned in relation to him. I want to know who they are and how they relate to his circumstances."

It was a tenuous thread. While he had no right to tell her not to go visit her father, he was running an active investigation. She suspected if he wanted to pull in the full weight of the NYPD he could find some way to manage it so that her father was unavailable today.

"You swear you're only asking him about known associates. Without any details on the safes?"

"Of course not."

"Then I guess it's a good thing I'm off duty for the next few days."

He must have seen the question in her eyes because he continued right on. "I'll drive you upstate to see him."

Wyatt was glad he and Marlowe were back on more even ground, but he couldn't deny that he'd done damage the night before with his reaction. He stood by it— his job required his absolute focus and after the attempt on him in the Hudson he could hardly afford to lose sight of that now.

But he still regretted the stilted conversation his actions had left behind.

"I hate this part of the drive," Marlowe murmured as Wyatt glanced at the GPS directions he had transmitting on his phone.

She hadn't said much and her words now felt a bit like a confession.

"Why do you hate it?"

"No matter how many times I come up here, this part's the worst. The highway signs began advertising there's a prison nearby and not to pick up hitchhikers."

Wyatt had seen those same signs starting about ten miles back. He'd noticed them—every prison he'd ever been to did the same—but he'd glossed over it as a matter of course.

"It's designed to protect people passing through. The ones who don't know there's a prison around."

"I know. It's just—" She broke off on a heavy sigh. "It's a sobering reality, you know? And proof that the pretty, rolling land outside these windows hides the home of maximum security criminals."

Wyatt knew there wasn't any answer he could give that would make that reality better for her, so he went with what was in his heart instead.

"I'm sorry you've had to live with this. That you've had to spend your adult life dealing with trips to prison. Even the other night's dinner with your mother. It's like this constant reminder of your father's choices."

"Thank you." She let out a harsh laugh, but under

it he heard the slightest quavers of vulnerability. "It's nicer than I can say to have someone acknowledge that."

They made the rest of the drive in silence, both wrapped in their own thoughts. The front desk wasn't that crowded and their IDs were processed in the visitor log quickly before they were escorted to the outside yard where Marlowe would meet with her father.

"I like it better in the warmer months. The outdoors." She gestured around to the prison yard after the guard who'd escorted them out had led them to a table. "The fresh air. It doesn't feel nearly as claustrophobic as in winter when you have to sit in those ugly little cubicles and talk on a phone."

As a cop he normally spent his prison visits with legal counsel inside rooms designed for the purposes of discussion and questioning. Now that he was out here, Wyatt could see how this sort of visit would be far easier on a prisoner's family than being stuck inside.

A light breeze whipped up, catching wisps of Marlowe's carefully styled and pinned-up hair. As he watched her smooth them back, he saw the slightest tremble in her hands; watched the way her eyes kept up a continual scan of the prison yard.

And saw that expressive gaze still when it landed on the tall, impressive-looking man in prison orange who crossed the yard toward them.

"Marlowe." Michael McCoy leaned in and pressed a kiss to his daughter's cheek. His hands were bound before him in cuffs but Marlowe reached up and wrapped her arms around his neck, pulling him close in a hug.

"Hi, Dad."

They stood there for another heartbeat before Marlowe pulled back, turning toward Wyatt. "I'd like to introduce you to a friend."

Wyatt ignored the handcuffs and extended a hand to Marlowe's father. "Mr. McCoy. I'm Wyatt."

He got the impression he'd done right by the handshake if the small note of satisfaction in the dark brown eyes, so like his daughter's, was any indication. And then the three of them settled themselves at a table with single seats around each side of the square, all bolted to the ground.

"I'm glad you're here, Lowe, but I was surprised to get the notice you were coming. I wasn't expecting you for a few more weeks."

"Your lawyer reached out with the details on your parole hearing. I wanted to talk to you about that and, well, a few other things."

Michael's gaze darted toward him and Wyatt got the distinct sense the man anticipated something personal. It was only when Marlowe continued on that Michael's curiosity shifted to a strange sort of resignation.

"I did some research into your case. I read a few transcripts and looked at some of the court notes."

"You did that years ago, Lowe. It's old news, baby."

"I read those notes as a teenager. Now I'm reading them as an adult. I was surprised to realize you had known associates. I thought you always worked alone."

Michael frowned at that. "I did work alone, most of my career."

If Marlowe was bothered by her father's reference to a life of theft as a "career" she didn't show it. Instead, she simply pressed on. "Why did you change to working with others?"

"When various parties catch word of your reputation, things begin to change all on their own. Those parties get interested in a man with my sort of skills. Speaking of parties—" Michael's gaze fell on Wyatt, a direct hit, before he continued. "Now I have some questions for you, Lowe. Including why you brought a cop with you today."

Marlowe left Michael's question hanging there, but Wyatt had to give her credit; she played it as cool as her father.

"Wyatt's working on something and he has questions. I do, too."

"And you weren't going to tell your dear old dad the real reason for your visit?"

"I'd say the fault is mine, sir." Wyatt stepped in. "I wasn't intending to deceive you. But I did want to get a sense of things before sharing my real reason for being here."

Once again, Wyatt got the distinct sense he was being measured up and meeting whatever standard Michael had, because the man nodded. "A sense of what things?"

"If I could trust you with my case."

"Something that involves me?" Michael glanced down at his cuffed hands before lifting his gaze, as well as his bound wrists. "I'm hardly in a position to make trouble."

"You're not the one I'm concerned with. But let's not pretend we both don't know word travels as fast in here as it does on the street." When Michael's gaze remained steady, Wyatt took it as agreement and continued on. "Marlowe was the one who made the connection. Between men you used to work with and some recently discovered elements in my case."

"You're working with the cops now, Lowe?" Michael did grin at that, a clear sense of amusement threading his words. "There's more of my father in you than I realized."

"I got pulled into this by circumstance. The NYPD uses my services."

"Ah, yes." Michael's tone turned grave, even as his smile remained firmly intact as he shifted his attention to Wyatt. "My daughter's fingers are as clever as mine. Shame she's been so determined to put them to less creative pursuits than I did."

Since Wyatt had seen the woman work, he wasn't sure Michael's assessment regarding her lack of creativity was accurate but he let it go. He was about to explain what they'd been looking at when Marlowe pressed on, a sudden urgency in her questions that hadn't been present since they'd sat down.

"Tell us about Harry Kisco and Mark Stone, Dad. What do you know about them?"

He'd already understood Marlowe wasn't unaffected by this visit, but that urgency spoke of as much of a desire to solve what was going on as Wyatt and the rest of his team. It was a reminder, once more, that her reasons for keeping Michael's known associates to herself might have been different than Wyatt's, but it wasn't because she wanted to hide anything.

She wanted answers, too.

"Dutch and Mark were some of those interested parties I mentioned."

"Dutch?" Marlowe probed.

"Harry's nickname." Michael waved a hand. "No idea where he got it, but that's what his friends called him. It's what he told me to call him."

"How interested were those guys?" Wyatt asked.

"Interested enough to drag me into a job or two, despite the independent nature of my work." Michael's gaze roamed over his daughter and in that look Wyatt saw all he needed to know.

Michael McCoy appeared invulnerable, but he was as human as the next person.

And Marlowe was likely the chink in his armor.

"They threatened to expose my work if I didn't help them on a job."

"And what about Nightwatch?" Wyatt pressed on.

"Their nightclub?" For the first time Michael looked surprised by the question. "They ran numbers out the back, but for all intents and purposes, it was a nightclub. One of their few legitimate businesses, actually. Well, aside from the illegal gambling, of course. But it was a hotspot for a few years before public sentiment had them closing and shifting their interests elsewhere."

"And that's all?"

Michael nodded. "That's all I remember."

Wyatt hadn't intended to lay all his cards on the table, but Michael's forthcoming responses—and no evidence of prevarication on the older man's part—had Wyatt pressing for more. "What does any of it have to do with an exhibit of jewels at the Natural History Museum."

"The one with the Burmese rubies?"

For a man who clearly knew how to keep his guard up, there was a surprising amount of amusement and openness in his features as they spoke. "That was a job.

A calling, really. I worked on that one for months, trying to find the angles to get in and get my shot at those jewels."

"Dad!"

Michael shrugged at the admonition. "Tried is the operative word. I never got my shot at them. The night I'd determined to go in and make my move the back entrance I'd been assured would be left open wasn't. I'd paid good money for that access but when I got there I was still locked out. When the window of time passed, I had to bug out. I didn't know then what happened and I never found out, either. But that job never happened for me."

"And you didn't go after your money?"

Michael shook his head. "I got wind about two weeks later that the accommodating guard who handled that door had retired, but he was just the lackey. Whoever was responsible got spooked and about a week after that I found an envelope with my full payment refunded in the mail."

"Dad, you have to know what this sounds like?"

"A simpler time, really." Michael's grin—and that charm Marlowe had spoken of was in full force—was broad as he shrugged his shoulders. "My work was to challenge me. I had no interest in being a common criminal or thug."

"A gentleman thief, you mean?" Wyatt asked.

Yet again, he was rewarded by the appreciation in the other man's gaze. "Yes, exactly that. I wanted the thrill of the hunt and the challenge of it all. Killing people or harming others was never in my wheelhouse."

It was one of the odder conversations he'd had in his career, yet in Michael's words, Wyatt got a sense of the man. His innate pride in his work as well as his belief that he wasn't a common criminal, despite his current circumstances.

Or, perhaps, Wyatt wondered, in spite of them.

His circumstances in the world, including two decades in prison, could have tarnished that view. It likely would have for most. Yet Michael's conviction was evident.

Even more so when his focus landed on Wyatt, his gaze direct, his words earnest.

"I know I hurt my family, Wyatt. I live with that every day. But I never behaved in a way that would hurt others. Their pocketbooks, maybe, but not them. Not in the places that really matter. But those men you spoke of?" Michael finally turned to look at his daughter. "They are the worst sort of criminal. They're the ones who prey on the innocent. Who have built their lives on the destruction of others."

"What do you know, Dad?"

"On your case, I'm afraid I'm no help. The Nightwatch nightclub closed years ago. I can't even imagine why it would be relevant now other than to say that yes, it existed for a time. But Harry and Mark? If they're involved in whatever you're dealing with?"

Michael leaned in across the table, his tone urgent. "If they're involved in this, you'd better watch your—"

Whatever he was about to say was cut off abruptly, his eyes going wide as he jerked in his chair.

His physical response was matched to the distinct ring of gunshots.

And as the screams registered around him, Marlowe's loudest of all, Wyatt moved into action, leaping out of his chair and covering her to keep her safe.

Chapter 14

Marlowe heard the screams, seemingly coming from outside of herself, before she realized they spilled from her throat.

More gunshots?

More chaos from a distance?

Directed at her father?

At that realization, she pressed against Wyatt, wanting to move. Needing to get to her father.

"Marlowe!"

Wyatt hollered through the commotion going on around them, several guards running through the courtyard while inmates who'd been in the yard ran back toward the main building.

"I need to get up. I need to see him."

The shots had stopped, the three that had rung out seemingly all that would come. Wyatt lifted himself off her and the moment she was free of his weight, she crawled around the table to her father.

Once more, that inhuman roar crawled up her throat but she managed to hold it back as she reached for him, a strange whimper falling from her lips as she dragged him into her lap.

"Daddy!" Blood spread outward on his prison uniform, the red dark and insidious against the bold orange of the jumpsuit.

"Marlowe, I have to go after—"

She glanced up to see Wyatt bouncing on the balls of his feet. "Go!"

"I'll get help!"

He raced off in the direction of the security station at the corner of the yard and she already heard the call over the intercom system for a medic.

Even as she feared it was a useless exercise.

"Dad. Stay with me. They're sending help."

Her father was still in her lap, his face contorted in pain as he wheezed shallow breaths.

"There's help coming, Daddy. Come on, you need to hang on."

"Lowe—" Her name came out on a gasp and she held him tight, wishing there was some way to comfort him. "I'm sorry, baby. Sorry I couldn't be—" He broke off on a hard exhale.

"Shh, don't try to talk."

"Need to…say…it."

She stilled as he laid a hand over hers where she tried to keep a palm over the bleeding that seemed to be everywhere. That endless, spreading dark over the front of his clothes.

"You deserved better. You always did. I'm sorry I couldn't give it to you. But I'm glad…" He let out a hard exhale. "I'm glad my dad could."

Marlowe kept up the pressure on his chest, but felt his breath slipping away all the same.

A team of medics arrived, gentle but firm as they tried to pull her away from her father.

"Ma'am. You need to let us work. You need—"

She let out a hard cry as she felt her father's body go limp in her arms.

"I don't think—"

One of the medics reached around her, obviously preparing to pull her father from her lap. She nearly held on, unwilling to let go, when she felt arms around her shoulders.

"Marlowe. Let them do their work."

The warmth of Wyatt's body struck her as he kept his arms around her. She let the medics take her father away and then allowed Wyatt to pull her close. It suddenly dawned on her how cold she was, the shivers gripping her with fierce claws.

"I'm sorry, Marlowe. I tried to catch him. I couldn't get out of the yard. I'm sorry, I—"

He stopped speaking as a hard sob escaped her lips and instead, just held her close, rocking her against his chest.

She cried and shivered as she watched them work on her father.

Even as she knew there was nothing now that could bring him back.

Wyatt coordinated with the local cops as well as the prison security team, but four hours after Michael

McCoy had been shot and killed they were no closer to getting answers.

The initial review of the crime scene had confirmed the shots came from a distance, outside the prison yard, in the hands of a long-range sniper. Beyond that, they had nothing.

He'd coordinated with Captain Reed and Arlo, the two of them working through some of the jurisdictional requirements needed to expand their case upstate. Because there was no question in anyone's mind McCoy's death was somehow related to the cases with the safes.

The issue was how anyone knew they were here.

He hadn't known Marlowe's intentions to visit the prison until seeing her that morning. And while he'd shared his credentials as part of his sign in at the prison, it wasn't like anyone had a heads-up he was accompanying her today.

Were they followed?

Was someone keeping tabs on McCoy's visitor logs? Marlowe had mentioned to her father when they were talking that she'd scheduled the trip, but that meant a hell of a lot of behind-the-scenes coordination by whoever was running this con.

One of the medics had taken care of Marlowe, giving her a place to get cleaned up and offering her an oversized T-shirt from a small stash of clean clothes they kept in reserve. When she came out to meet him the shirt hung to the middle of her thighs. Something about that look—the way the material dwarfed her— had a hard fist lodging in his chest.

It was time to get her home.

He wrapped up the last few conversations he needed to

have, adding the promise that he and Arlo would be back up in the morning, and then walked over to Marlowe.

"Come on. I'll drive you home."

She allowed him to take her arm, leading her back out past the entry and on to the car. In minutes they were back on the road, the pretty land around the Hudson River an odd backdrop to all the horror they'd witnessed today.

"I still don't believe it." She murmured the words after they'd been in the car about twenty minutes. He'd cleared the town that held the prison and had driven by a few more towns so that those signs she'd mentioned earlier—not to pick up hitchhikers—had finally faded away.

"I'm sorry, Marlowe. I'm so sorry for your loss."

"He was so close to parole. I really thought he'd get it this time, too, you know? Served his debt to society and all that." She shook her head, her gaze on the land that passed outside the passenger-side window. "No longer a threat to the public and able to serve the rest of his time under a supervised schedule."

Wyatt kept shifting his gaze from the road to her and back again. "Based on the man I met today he had a good shot at it."

"And my grandfather. I have to tell him. And—" She broke off on a hard sob. "He said he was sorry. There at the end, when he could barely speak, he told me he was sorry that he couldn't be what I needed him to be."

"You don't have to figure all this out now, Marlowe. You deserve the time to take it in."

He reached over and took her hand, pleased when she held on through the tears. It wasn't much but a sign that maybe they could get back to that place where they'd been. That place where she trusted him.

The afternoon traffic back into the city was heavy and Marlowe's sobs tapered off as they drove. But in their place was a quiet heaviness that permeated the air.

What did all of this have to do with her father?

And why now?

Until the connection last night when Marlowe showed Wyatt the internet photo of Harry and Mark in front of the Nightwatch club, Michael McCoy wasn't even on their radar as part of the problem. Now less than twenty-four hours later the man's dead?

Wyatt played the case through in his mind. The first three safes had kept them all focused on the murders but looking back on it now, maybe that was the whole point. The fact that the three men were entirely unrelated and had no connection to one another increasingly seemed like the point.

Marlowe had used the term escalation when she referred to the fourth safe, over breakfast with Anderson, and it was so strange to look at it now and realize that's exactly what that fourth safe had been.

Burying the safe at the base of the bridge was deliberate. It amped up the stakes and the entire case changed and shifted with that choice.

The contents inside.

The attack on him during the Hudson River dive.

And now Michael's murder.

"I keep going over it and over it in my mind," Marlowe said.

Her voice was husky from crying and he reached for

her hand again, squeezing her fingers in his. "It's under-standable. It's all new and you're trying to process it."

"How did they know we'd be there? And how'd they know we'd sit there?" she asked. "Right there? We could have been anywhere in that yard, yet we were some-where in shooting distance?"

"Say that again."

"That we could have been anywhere?"

Wyatt had gone over the scene in his mind, too, something lingering that wasn't entirely clear. Her refer-ence to where they sat clicked a few thoughts into place.

"When I walked the exterior of the prison yard with the local police there were only a few specific places the shooter could have used, even with a long-range scope on the rifle."

"What are you saying, Wyatt?"

Excitement built, a sense that something—finally something—might give them a clue. "The table. When the guard gestured us where to sit. Did he give us a specific seat?"

"He directed us to that table." The heavy weight that had lain over her shoulders faded in the face of his ques-tions and she sat up straighter. "I didn't think of it at the time but he very clearly directed us to that seat when he showed us to the yard."

"That's my memory, too."

Wyatt cycled through it again. Their stop at the front desk to check in and give their IDs. The guard who es-corted them outside. Even the way he'd gestured to the table. He'd been casual, but specific in his guidance and since they'd had no reason to question it, they'd taken the seats he suggested.

"I need to call this in."

Wyatt dug the number out of his breast pocket from the detective he'd met from the local precinct and quickly explained to her the remembered walk out to the yard. She asked him a few questions and Wyatt fact-checked his memories with Marlowe, but by the time he'd hung up, he had her very real promise to get back to the prison to ask questions of every guard who'd been on duty.

"That was really good thinking," Wyatt affirmed once he'd hung up. "Detective Adams confirmed there were minimal sight lines outside the prison yard."

"Meaning?"

"Meaning a sniper, no matter how good, didn't have a shot all over the prison yard. There were limited positions and we were placed in one of them."

"Wyatt," she exhaled, her voice quivering again with tears. "He's dead because I went up there today. If I'd only have told you what I thought you could have handled it. I should have left you to do your job. Why did I need to see him? Why did I do this?"

"You didn't do this, Marlowe. A criminal with a deadly purpose did this."

"But if I'd have left it alone. Why did I think it was okay to do this? To go up there and ask him questions and play freaking detective!"

The tears she'd gotten under control rose up again, her sobs hard and heavy as she shed her grief. He wanted to comfort her, but he knew there wasn't a thing he could say to help her past this beyond giving her a safe place to get it out.

He didn't agree with her assessment—and when

things weren't as fresh he'd make sure she knew—but Michael McCoy wasn't killed because his daughter went to visit him in prison. He was killed today so he couldn't help his daughter and her NYPD accompaniment figure out what was at the heart of the case that had more twists, turns and curves than the Hudson.

Worse, Michael was killed because he was a loose end.

Wyatt didn't know all the details yet, but he knew to the depths of his soul that he was right.

For now, it was his job to figure out why.

Carson Booth drove out of the employee parking lot at the prison and headed for the small meeting place at a highway rest stop about four exits down. He'd been wary at first of meeting in the open, but the guys who hired him had been fair and decent so far. Besides, it was late afternoon, the sun was still high in the sky and he carried a gun in his glove box.

What could possibly happen?

He'd gotten the first payment, just for meeting, just as promised. The second had come when all he'd had to do was nose around the visitor log files and share some information. Today, he'd collect payment number three.

And only for suggesting to a few guests up visiting the prison where to sit in the yard.

He felt bad about the outcome, but how was he to know the seats at that table were visible off the property? He'd been paid to do a job and the whys of it were none of his business. And one fewer inmate was good for the taxpayers, right?

Besides, if he played his cards right, he could get

more of these jobs. Who gave a rat's butt about the prisoners inside anyway? They'd just as soon turn on him if he so much as eyed someone sideways. No reason he couldn't make some good money on the side for spending all day working in that hellhole.

He took the exit for the rest area, pulling off into the long parking lot with diagonally drawn spots. The place had a few cars and he went to the far end, taking a spot near the picnic tables that overlooked a view of the river. A small building housed the restrooms and vending machines, but Carson was careful to stay far away from the building and any of the cameras that set at the corners of the structure.

The picnic tables were empty and he crossed over to the last one, taking a seat like he'd been told. If this drop followed the same as the first two, he'd get a call after he'd sat down and would be given additional directions from there.

He'd barely sat, squinting his eyes from the glare reflecting off the water, when his phone rang.

"Booth here."

"Mr. Booth. Thank you for your service today."

"I did the job as asked."

"Yes, you did. Perfectly, as a matter of fact. If you lean down and feel under the picnic table, you'll find your payment."

Carson bent to the side, his hand stretching to probe the underside of the table. Just as his contact suggested, Carson felt a thick envelope taped around the midsection of the wooden planks. His fingers closed over it, the peeling of tape audible as he pulled off the thick package.

He'd been promised a thousand dollars for this job and had requested it in twenties. But as his hand closed on the envelope, it felt like a lot more in there.

An additional advance for future work?

He couldn't wait to open it up.

It was the last thought Carson Booth would ever have as one single shot rang out, the bullet embedding itself in the back of his skull.

As his hand reflexively closed over the envelope, left intentionally unsealed, a slew of paper money from a board game flew out of the envelope, picked up on the light breeze drifting over the Hudson.

Marlowe couldn't believe her father was gone. The man who'd occupied such a complex and complicated place in her life was still her father.

Still someone she loved very much.

And now he was gone.

Wyatt hadn't indulged her line of thinking about asking questions, but she was at fault.

She'd made the trip today.

She'd asked the questions.

She'd requested the meeting that killed him.

The drive back into the city had seemed endless as they'd waded through late afternoon traffic and it was almost seven by the time they pulled up to her grandfather's street. She'd requested that the police leave the responsibility for telling Anderson McCoy that his son was dead to her.

And now that she was here, about to tell him, Marlowe couldn't deny the mounting sense of dread that filled her bloodstream and curdled her empty stomach.

If she had a complicated relationship with her father it was nothing compared to the one Anderson had for his son. The love of a father combined with the disappointment of a parent.

As she'd told Wyatt, she rarely spoke of her father with her grandfather. For as much as they could discuss, the subject of his son had always been oddly off-limits with Pops.

Only now, on this one thing, she had no choice.

You can do this.

The mental pep talk—one she'd given herself off and on during the two-hour drive—floated through her mind, even as she had a hard time believing those words.

Wyatt came around the car, reaching for her hand. "Come on. We'll do this together."

They headed up the short walkway to the front door and Marlowe suddenly realized what she was wearing. The medic who'd checked her out had kindly offered her the clean T-shirt as she discarded her own blood-covered one. Staring down now, at the shirt that came well past her waist, brought the sense memory back of seeing herself in the prison bathroom mirror, covered in blood.

An involuntary shiver raced down her back.

Would she ever not see it?

Wyatt's large hand still enveloped her own and she tried to focus on the warm strength there and not on the terrible images that had forced their way into her thoughts all afternoon.

Marlowe had debated letting herself in with her key but since she hadn't wanted to give him advance warning they were coming, she knocked on the door, giving him the courtesy of answering. His smile was broad as he opened the door, the welcome falling as he caught sight of them.

"What happened?"

"Pops, I—" She moved into his arms, pulling him close. "Pops, I'm sorry."

"Michael." His arms went around her. "It's Michael."

She nodded, laying her cheek against his shoulder. "It's Dad. He's gone."

They stood like that a long time, his questions coming out in short bursts and her answers a jumbled mix of memories and facts that, bit by bit, told him what had happened that afternoon.

Wyatt had eventually moved them into the living room to sit down before heading into the kitchen to make coffee.

"Lowe, this can't be true."

"I know." She held his hand, the skin of his fingertips worn smooth. "I keep thinking it's a bad dream."

"I didn't even know you were going up to the prison this week."

Another wave of guilt hit her. The continued idea that she'd brought this upon her father by virtue of her visit striking a hard note in her chest.

"I did this. My determination to get answers."

"What answers?"

"The case, Pops. Wyatt's case involves Dad somehow and I wanted to know more."

"You don't need to be messing around in police work, Lowe."

For the first time since she'd uttered the words that

her father was gone, something filtered through the clear grief in Pops's eyes.

"I needed to know if he knew anything. If this related to him." She took a hard breath. "Now, with this outcome? How can it not?"

"You don't need to know anything. You need to leave the work to the cops."

"He's my father."

The mulish expression that had settled on her grandfather's face twisted into a mask of pain and anger. "You're not a cop. This doesn't involve you!"

"Pops! This does involve me. It involves all of us now."

Her grandfather's outburst was a surprise, but as more bitter, hard-edged words filled the space between them on the couch, she realized there was so much more going on that she never understood.

Worse, that she couldn't have imagined.

"No, it doesn't. It can't involve you. I kept Michael safe. I made sure of that."

"You made sure of what?"

Marlowe had known this would be a difficult conversation—how could it be anything else? But as she sat there, taking in the stooped lines of her grandfather's still-broad shoulders and the obstinate set to his mouth, she saw something else.

That disappointed parent she believed she knew—that she'd believed was the very definition of his relationship with Michael—had more facets than she could have ever imagined.

"What did you make sure of, Mr. McCoy?"

Wyatt settled two mugs down on the coffee table

before taking a seat in the well-worn chair her grandfather used to watch TV.

"I handled it. I made sure he was safe."

"Pops, what are you talking about?"

"That was my job. I'm his father and he refused to see that his work, as he called it, was a dead end. It was a destructive streak I never understood. But I had to fix it."

Grief and anger swirled like a storm underneath his words. Her father had been in jail for more than a decade, yet as she listened to her grandfather it was as if it had happened mere days before, the pain still so fresh.

"Why don't you take us through it from the beginning?"

Wyatt's voice was gentle when he spoke, but he asked the question with the clear expectation of receiving answers.

"I fixed it. Years ago, I fixed it all. I deliberately looked the other way in exchange for them to leave Michael alone. They used my son against me but I made the choices I needed to so I could keep him safe." Pops turned his gaze on her, pleading. "So I could keep you safe."

"Safe from what?"

"They wanted to use him. They wanted his skills to run the neighborhood. They would have found you, too."

Although he'd only half answered Wyatt's question, Marlowe began to put the various elements together.

Her grandfather's strange reaction when Wyatt had told him the contents of the fourth safe.

That lingering guilt he seemed to carry when she did bring up the subject of her father, cloaked in terse answers and as minimal a response as possible, obviously designed to change the topic.

Her grandfather's reputation was sterling, a testament to his work ethic and deep sense of honor.

It was overwhelming to realize her father's crimes had somehow ruined both.

Chapter 15

Wyatt gave them a moment to talk, heading back into the kitchen to retrieve his own cup of coffee. It was a simple task, but he sensed that Marlowe needed the moment of quiet to process yet one more crack in the foundation of her life.

Hell, he needed a minute to process it. A fact that became evident as coffee sloshed over the rim of his mug when he poured too much in distraction.

He cleaned up the small mess with a paper towel and considered what he knew.

What "protection" Anderson spoke of?

And what Anderson had done to keep Marlowe safe?

There was only one way to fully know and as he headed back into the living room, Wyatt recognized the best way to get the answers he needed was *through*.

Through pain and grief and a history that refused to stay buried.

"When we spoke the other day, sir, you seemed distracted. Am I correct in thinking that you did know what Nightwatch was?"

Anderson's stare was direct, no hint of the prevarication or distraction he'd shown the other morning. "I do. It was a nightclub down along the water. Two guys who ran it fancied themselves as businessmen but they were using the club as a front."

Michael had told them as much earlier, but Wyatt let Anderson tell the story, curious to understand how many details matched.

"A front for what?"

"Gambling mostly. Vice had kept a close eye on it when it first opened but I smoothed the way, made sure those eyes turned elsewhere. I was the chief of detectives at the time. I could shift and direct their focus as needed."

"And in exchange?"

"In exchange, they kept Michael out of their plans. They'd marked him for a few local jobs they needed his skills on but I made sure they left him alone as part of our deal."

"But Dad worked alone," Marlowe pressed.

"He thought that, too. And he spent most of his life managing just fine on his own. But he was in the game too long. Sooner or later, Lowe, skills like your father's get attention."

Anderson shook his head. "I hated thinking of him that way, but he was skilled at what he did. There was an aptitude there and, much as I hated to acknowledge it, I also understood why he didn't manage to stay under the radar."

That description—of skills in demand—had Wyatt thinking about the faceless sniper who'd shot at him and Marlowe, as well as Michael. And the diver who'd tried to take him out.

Were they one and the same?

That belief they were dealing with highly skilled ex-military persisted, as did the idea that they were dealing with criminals who knew how to keep a variety of those skilled professionals on hand.

Tools to meet an end, Wyatt realized.

"What about the other details in the safe? The article from the *Times* and the diner receipt and the parking ticket?"

"Michael was aiming for that exhibit. He wanted a shot at those jewels and I was afraid he'd do it, too."

"We asked Dad earlier." Marlowe recounted the discussion for her grandfather. "He said that he wanted a shot at it, too, but the back door wasn't open. That was his way in, the one he'd planned for, and it was blocked."

"That was their payment to me. Proof they could cut a gentleman's agreement if I looked the other way on their crimes. The diner was where we made the deal and the parking ticket is a message, I think."

"A message about what?" Wyatt asked.

"It was the first thing I overlooked. One of the nightclub owner's cars was double-parked. The ticket was the first small test."

Wyatt couldn't help but be fascinated by the entire operation. He and the team had batted a lot of theories around, but that sense of a game had been present from the start. But as he considered Anderson's retelling, Wyatt had to admit that the layers and nuance were amazing, like a large chessboard with various pieces all in motion.

Pieces that had sat on that board for a hell of a long time.

He was about to say as much when his phone rang. The number matched the one for Detective Adams he'd put into his phone earlier and he excused himself to take the call in the kitchen.

"Trumball."

"Detective Trumball. It's Olivia Adams. I followed up on the prison guard we discussed."

"Did you find anything?"

"Yes, his body about an hour ago. It's not verified yet, but I'd bet my badge the ballistics are going to come back a match for the gun used on Michael McCoy."

She walked him through the discovery of the body by a traumatized couple at a rest stop not far from the prison. But the method of death—another execution from a distance—once again spoke of a military exercise.

They discussed a few more details and he promised follow up from Captain Reed the next day before disconnecting the call.

As he walked back into the living room, Wyatt acknowledged the truth.

One more chess piece had moved on the board.

Marlowe hadn't wanted to leave her grandfather, but exhaustion finally took over around ten. Pops promised he'd be fine and claimed he wanted a bit of quiet time of his own.

"I need some time to think, Lowe. Wyatt." He'd nodded. "I'll be calling Dwayne in the morning."

"He'll come here, sir. You don't have to go into the precinct."

Her grandfather looked like he'd aged a decade since she and Wyatt had arrived, but his head was held high when he finally spoke. "I'll go see Captain Reed myself. It's the least I can do."

It was all she'd have ever expected of him, too, Marlowe thought as Wyatt drove her home. Even as her heart broke for the news he had to share. His reputation and a lifetime of work would be destroyed with the news of what he'd done.

One more facet of the devastation that was her father's life.

It pained her to think like that, but even through the pain, she couldn't extinguish the steady flame of anger, either.

How many lives were affected by her father's crimes? Even the dead guard discovered earlier. Yes, he'd made his choices and had obviously paid for it with his life, but it was also one more life lost in this entire mess that spanned decades.

More death and destruction and waste.

She'd spent a lot of years battling different opinions. About her family and her work. From the quiet gossip about her father's crimes to the questioning eyebrow raises at her own chosen profession, people had always had opinions. They'd ranged from outright suspicion to subtle amusement to clear support and the "good path" she'd chosen to build her own business.

All of it, including that subtly embarrassing sense of being watched, was because of her father.

"What are you thinking about?" Wyatt asked as they pulled up under a streetlamp about a block from her building.

She turned to him, his features outlined in sharp relief by the bright glow of halogen. "Other people's perceptions."

"People have a lot of them."

She reached for the car handle before thinking better of it. "Whatever people think about my grandfather? That's all going to change."

"Some."

She saw the hesitation there but was oddly grateful he didn't try to breeze through it, even with a polite lie. "Sadly, a lot. I think he knows that."

"Cops are a tough lot, but they know the job. Don't underestimate people's ability to understand the impossible choice your grandfather was dealing with."

"You're kind, Wyatt. The fact you can still say that, even with all we saw today, is a testament to your character. But it wasn't only my father who died today. My grandfather's reputation died along with it."

He looked about to argue with her before he tilted his head toward her front door. "Why don't we go inside? It's been a long day."

"You don't have to stay."

"I'm not leaving you alone. There's still a threat out there."

"I appreciate it but really, you don't need to stay. Whatever the threat, it's not directed at me."

He ignored that, getting out of the car and coming around to open her door. She swung a leg out when she realized he still loomed over the open door, staring down at her. "Did you forget what happened as we walked out of dinner the other night?"

"But it's not me they want."

"You don't know that, Marlowe. And I'm not taking the risk."

He gave her the space to get out and she considered arguing but she was so tired. And sad. And…

"My mom! God, how could I have forgotten to call her?"

The thought of calling her mother got her moving, pushing away the exhaustion and the brewing argument with Wyatt as she headed for the front door of her building.

Even if he did seem rather immovable on the subject of staying. And if the idea of having him close left her with a sense of safety and security that she hadn't fully come to on her own?

Well, she'd think about that later when she wasn't so upside down with her emotions and so needy for these feelings for him that had only grown as the day progressed.

They'd started out this morning with a huge chasm between them. One she'd fully expected would slow down or completely shut off the tentative relationship building between them. But as they'd spent time together—as he protected her once again from forces outside of them— they'd been more partners than adversaries.

It was something she wanted, she admitted to herself. Even in the midst of all the upheaval in her life, she wanted to see where this relationship went.

But those were thoughts for another time.

For now, she needed to be responsible to another relationship.

Marlowe had her phone out by the time she and Wyatt got into her apartment and dialed her mother, suddenly at a loss for words once Patty answered the call.

"Darling!" Her mother's happy voice echoed from the phone and Marlowe had the overwhelming sense of what she had to do.

Of the news she had to deliver.

"Um, hi, Mom."

"Sweetheart? What's wrong?"

"Well, I'm sorry but…well, something happened today."

"Marlowe?"

"Dad died."

That truth—so hard to say—was finally out.

"He what? How? Michael?"

The tears she'd managed to hold back most of the day burst through the layers of numb she'd cloaked herself in. Wyatt moved in immediately, grabbing the phone from her hand and taking over the call to her mother.

"Patty. It's Wyatt."

Marlowe abstractly heard him walk her mother through the details as she took a seat on the couch. He was straightforward in the retelling, but kind, as he went over and then repeated information a few times to her mother's obvious questions.

"Why don't I have her call you tomorrow, Patty, if that's alright?"

Her mother must have agreed because after a soft goodbye, Wyatt crossed the room and laid her phone on the coffee table.

"I'm sorry."

"Don't be. She's got the information now and will talk to you tomorrow."

"I don't know why I couldn't tell her." She glanced up at Wyatt from where she sat on the couch with a shrug. "Maybe more of that family dysfunction I've managed to show you in every way?"

"There's no shame in being sad. None at all."

"I'm not ashamed of the sad, Wyatt. It's all the rest that's the rub."

The idea settled in, picking up a serious head of steam as she began to list her reasons.

"Mother deceiving her new beau. My father shot in a prison yard. And my grandfather lying to a precinct of people who've revered him for decades. Just a regular old day in the McCoy household."

Her voice cracked on the last, more tears spilling out to mix with the seething anger she couldn't seem to burn out of her system.

She'd carried it, in some way, for the majority of her life. That steady, simmering fury that the people around her—the people tasked to protect her and care for her—were so unwilling to put her first.

But this news about her grandfather had taken that low-level simmer and seemingly exploded it.

Which made the strong arms that pulled her close such a revelation. As she laid her head on his chest, settling in against him, Marlowe felt the first, subtle loosening of those tight, furious fists around her spine.

And allowed herself to land in a soft, warm, welcome space.

Wyatt held Marlowe close and let the range of emotions spill from her, one after another. She cycled through tears more than a few times, but the subtle yet steady loosening of her body as the time passed assured him she was processing the wild mix of feelings that she'd spent the day bearing up under.

Hell, that she'd spent a lifetime hauling on her shoulders.

Whatever lingering anger of his own over the internet photos she'd discovered had faded away. Although he'd have preferred she came to him first, the afternoon had reinforced for him that she was in an untenable position.

And that her family held a greater hold over her than she perhaps wanted to acknowledge.

It was a situation he understood…deeply.

He carried the burden of his own father's death and the resentment that still filled him over his mother and brother's decisions. It was family dynamics—the good and the bad.

"I can't believe he's gone."

Marlowe had been quiet for a while and her crying spell had left her voice throaty and raw.

"It's shock and grief. Give yourself time to process it."

"I've always loved him, but I guess I'd always thought that losing him would be easy, somehow. Or easier, maybe, since he's not an active part of my life." She shifted against his chest, staring up at him. "Now I see how badly I'd deluded myself."

"It's not a delusion. You've had to protect yourself and find a way to reconcile the person you love with the person who's made very poor choices. That's not an easy middle ground to exist in."

"It's going to be the hardest on my grandfather."

Since he'd worried about the same, Wyatt tried to encourage as best he could. "He's tough and he's got you."

Wyatt could only hope there wouldn't be too much fall out from Anderson's decisions so many years ago. The statute of limitations on nearly any crimes that would have happened at the time Nightwatch was an active club had long run out. Even so, no matter how long ago it had happened, the news of a chief of detectives looking the other way would still cast aspersions on the NYPD, especially if spun correctly by ambitious politicians or legal teams.

It was a bridge they'd cross once Anderson talked to the captain. Until then, Wyatt needed to keep his full focus on Marlowe.

For all her bravado in the car, dismissing his protection, he wasn't fully comfortable that there wasn't an external threat to her still out there lurking. It was unlikely, her position so close to Michael in the prison yard making both of them easy targets to a trained sniper, but he didn't want to take chances.

"Thank you for staying again tonight."

"You're welcome."

She still stared up at him and Wyatt recognized the unique torture of protecting her.

He wanted this woman.

And despite all that had happened the past few days, his feelings had been building for quite some time.

She lifted a hand, her fingers tracing a path over his jaw. "Thank you for today. For being there. I don't know what I would have done if I was up at the prison alone."

"You don't need to thank me for—"

She shifted her thumb to press against his lips. "Thank you."

He just nodded at that, pressing his lips in a kiss against the pad of her thumb.

They sat like that for several breaths, their gazes locked, and for a few moments the heartbreaking malevolence of the day drifted away. It didn't vanish, but they got some respite from it in that all-encompassing heat between them.

He got the sense Marlowe was going to say something when she seemingly thought better of it, tucking her head against his chest.

For as much as he wanted her, Wyatt realized, he wanted this, too. That sense of having a partner at the end of the day. Someone to share it all with, even overwhelming and difficult days.

She'd come to his home the night before when she'd heard the news of his attack in the Hudson. And while he'd sent her away over Nightwatch, before that revelation he'd been grateful she was there.

Her very presence had made his nerves after the attack better.

Now, tonight, he only hoped he could do the same for her.

And as her breathing deepened and evened out as she lay against his chest, Wyatt realized one more truth.

She was the person he wanted to share his days and nights with. Because in an incredibly short period of time, she'd come to mean everything to him.

Marlowe came awake on a heavy rush, the weight around her midsection stifling. She nearly flopped off the couch until she finally realized she was about to struggle against a person.

A very warm person in the form of Wyatt.

Had they slept here? All night?

Since the last she remembered was laying her head back against his chest and now it was morning, it seemed entirely true, but why hadn't either of them woken up?

Which brought the second wave of memory flooding over her like a dam let loose.

Her father.

And the heartbreaking grief that he wasn't simply gone, but that he'd been taken in such a violent show of revenge.

She'd managed to put it out of her mind for a few hours, but there was so much still to do. Including a follow-up call to her mother to talk to Patty herself and a check in on her grandfather before he headed into the precinct to talk to Dwayne.

Catching herself, Marlowe waited, allowing the physical safety she felt in Wyatt's arms battle against the roiling thoughts and the emotional turmoil that refused to fully settle. As her breathing calmed, she decided to take full advantage of the large, firm chest she still lay against and simply be present for a few minutes.

After all, it wasn't every morning a woman woke up

in such capable, strong arms. She and Wyatt had both been running on fumes, her father's murder and Wyatt's attack in the harbor on his dive having left them with very few defenses and minimal rest. Probably why they'd both dropped into an exhausted sleep.

Would it be so bad to give in and just take the physical for a while?

As she once again allowed herself to feel—the physical strength of the body that lay pressed against hers, the deeply male scent that hinted at the sea and the light scratch of whiskers against her forehead where she'd brushed against his chin—Marlowe allowed herself the fantasy of what could be.

And came to a decision.

For all the turmoil and upheaval in her life, she wanted this.

She wanted what was between them.

"Do you always think this loudly in the morning?"

The husky rumble of his voice, the cadence of it where his chest pressed against hers, had Marlowe nearly scrambling out of his arms like a wet cat. Clever as ever, he seemed to sense her actions before she did, tightening his arms around her before she could move.

"Going somewhere?"

"I just—" She brushed her hair behind her ears, suddenly conscious of how she looked. "I'm probably getting heavy and I'm sorry I woke you up."

"I'm not."

The words were sexy—the warm welcome in his eyes even more so—but he released his hold and she scrambled up to a sitting position.

"I can make coffee."

He grabbed her hand before she could get up and off the couch. "I was only teasing you about thinking out loud. Take the time to wake up."

For all her bravado as she'd laid there in his arms, a sudden sweep of nerves raced through her. They were attracted to each other—that hadn't been a secret—but what was the protocol to initiate sex after several traumatic days of heavy danger and emotional pain?

Was it crass? Opportunistic?

Or did it just come off needy?

Vowing to figure it out after brushing her teeth and fixing coffee, she got off the couch. "I'm just going to freshen up."

When he said nothing else, his gaze unreadable, she headed off to do both.

And was still considering the balance of danger and neediness fifteen minutes later as the coffee maker gave out its final gurgle, signaling a full pot.

Her apartment kitchen was surprisingly large for a one-bedroom apartment in Brooklyn, the room big enough to hold a small drop-leaf table for two. But just like the other morning when he'd woken up in her home, the space suddenly felt small and much too close when Wyatt walked into the kitchen. The twin scents of soap and toothpaste followed him, and she could see he'd washed his face, the front of his hair still sticking up in wet spikes.

Goodness, the man was adorable. Large and sexy and powerful and still, there was something sweet about those wet spikes. A small nod to what she imagined he'd looked like as a little boy.

"I can run out and get us some breakfast," he said,

picking up the mug she'd set out for him on the small table.

"You don't have to bother. I have eggs or toast and I always keep a few bagels in the freezer we can defrost."

"Spoken like a true New Yorker."

"They are carb-laden perfection."

She'd already fixed her own mug and had just turned away from the counter to go to the fridge when his hand reached for hers, stilling her movement. "Are you upset I'm here? I got the sense the other morning it was awkward and I can feel it again. You don't have to make me breakfast or pour me coffee. I don't have any expectations of you, Marlowe. I'm here to watch out for you."

Wasn't that the problem?

She glanced down where their hands linked and struggled with the best way to play this.

And realized, after all they'd been through, the only real answer was the truth.

Looking up from their joined hands into his eyes, she said the words that had lived in her mind for a while now. "I want you."

He kept their hands joined as he moved closer to her, stopping just shy of their bodies touching, yet close enough that she could feel all that glorious heat. His face was serious, those blue eyes drawing her in. "That's not why I stayed."

"I know."

"Good." He moved those last few inches so that their bodies were flush against each other, his other hand going around her back to pull her close. "Because I want you, too."

Their mouths met, those hints of coffee and toothpaste sweetly endearing and domestic before the kiss turned incendiary. Heat and need and raw electricity arced between them as Wyatt deepened the kiss. She met him, her arms tightening around him as she allowed him greater access, their tongues mating in a carnal preview of all to come.

Long, sensual moments spun out, an enticing mix of lazy exploration and driving need that dueled for dominance. It was only as Wyatt stilled their kiss, his lips curving into a smile against her mouth that Marlowe realized the scales had tipped toward driving need.

"I'm not at all suggesting an aversion to kitchen sex, but maybe we could move into the bedroom for our first time together?"

"I think we can do that." She moved back, her smile broad. "You sure you don't want me to fix you that bagel first?"

His face fell for the briefest moment before he caught the joke, diving for her and taking her in another hard kiss before he began moving them determinedly toward the bedroom. Clothes fell to the floor as they moved from the kitchen, down the short hallway to her bedroom, so that by the time they got to her bed, they were naked.

He kissed her down onto the bed, following so that he covered her with his body. Marlowe reveled in the things he did to her, his lips moving over her flesh like a caress. From the sensitive area behind her ear to light kisses over her shoulder to the fiery moments he took her nipple between his lips, each step in his exploration was a gift.

And as sighs grew deeper, breathier, she went on an

exploration of her own. Hard planes of muscle flexed under her fingers as she ran her hands down his back. She knew he was well-built—the demands of his job ensured it—but the body beneath her fingers was a work of art.

Long, firm muscles. Slim hips. Sculptured shoulders. Every bit of him was perfect.

Suddenly impatient for more, her hand slipped between them, reaching for the hard length of him. She knew the moment firm strokes gave her the upper hand and she used his hard intake of breath to shift their positions, rolling him onto his back so she could straddle him.

Those firm strokes grew longer, bolder, and Wyatt's breaths grew more shallow as she put his body through the most delicious paces. And just when she was convinced she'd won the round, he neatly turned the tables on her, slipping his hand between them to stroke the most intimate part of her.

"Wyatt—" His name exhaled on a soft moan as he worked her sensitive flesh, tension building with each moment.

In a beautiful explosion of need and the deepest arousal she'd ever experienced, her body shuddered around him. Wyatt pulled her close as he rode her through her orgasm, whispering sexy words of appreciation before he kissed her.

Had she ever…?

How had he…?

Marlowe's thoughts drifted with the waves of pleasure and she reveled in his touch. As he gathered her close against him, his arms cradling her, she felt her body stirring once more, shocked she could be ready so quickly.

And yet, as she looked down at the firm lines of his sexy, stubbled jaw, she knew there was so much more to discover.

So much more to experience.

Together.

Pressing her lips to his ear, she whispered, "Why don't you reach into my end table over there."

He grinned down at her, even as his hand was already snaking over to the drawer.

"It's hard to argue with a prepared woman," Wyatt said as he pulled a condom from the drawer. "And right now I'd like to add extra heaps of praise since I arrived unprepared."

"Then it's sure to be a most excellent morning for both of us."

Snagging the condom from his hand, she made quick work of the package and unrolled it over the hard length of him, adding an additional stroke of her palm against the underside of his erection for good measure. Not to be outdone, he quickly flipped her onto her back, rising up over her to fit his body intimately to hers.

She'd known they'd fit, but it happened so easily. So perfectly.

And as he began to move, long, sure, smooth strokes in perfect rhythm, Marlowe gave herself up to the moment.

To Wyatt.

And to this beautiful connection between them.

Chapter 16

Wyatt wondered if he had to open his eyes and decided a man who'd just seen the heavens explode was entitled to a few more minutes of reverent silence. Since keeping his eyes closed had the added benefit of giving him a few more moments to simply savor every last drop of what it had meant to make love with Marlowe, Wyatt figured he had the right of it.

God, she was amazing. And not just because they'd started the day with what had to be the best sex of his life, but because she was warm, generous and giving.

All he'd imagined—and he'd imagined quite a bit—and so much more.

She'd curled up next to him as they'd both drifted on the afterglow before kissing him gently on the cheek a short while ago and slipping from the bed. He thought to call her back when her voice drifted to the bedroom, the greeting to her mother clear enough.

He opted to give her the space to make the call, but did keep an ear to the conversation, ready to step in if she needed his help once more.

Unlike last night, her voice had the quiet, confident notes he associated with her.

And also unlike last night, she was able to get through the conversation with her mother, even if he heard the telltale notes of tears lacing her voice.

Wyatt wished he could do something for her to make this better, but he knew the only way to deal with the loss of a parent was, sadly, to deal with it. More bad days than good at first, along with waves of grief that swamped you at unexpected times.

He'd been a teenager when he'd experienced it, yet he could still conjure those feelings. Hell, he even felt them now from time to time, a reminder those waves could still pack a powerful punch.

But the violent way she lost her father would place an added dimension on that grief.

He'd be there for her and he'd help her through it. And as that mental assurance floated through his mind, Wyatt realized one more thing.

He wanted to be there, by her side. Now and in the future.

A large part of him—the one who'd never been all that successful at long-term relationships—wondered when a sense of panic was going to set in at the mere notion of sticking around past a few more weeks or months.

And the part of him that had reveled in spending time

with Marlowe, from that very first night over pie at her grandfather's, realized he wanted to stay.

He rolled that over in his mind, pleased to realize just how well it fit.

Maybe it's because of how well he fit with Marlowe.

The idea took root, settling in, but before he could think too long on it, Marlowe walked back into the room.

"Are you okay? How'd it go with your mom?"

"It was fine. She's still in shock." Marlowe sighed as she crossed to stand beside the bed. "And I know I'm being a bad person. She did love him once. But somehow the call ended up being all about her. How devastated she is and how she never got to say goodbye."

"What about how much she cares for Brock?"

"Never came up."

Wyatt had a career built on the oddities of human behavior, more of it bad than good. He chalked up much of what he saw and experienced professionally to the worst impulses people were capable of.

Yet it stung in a different way when he saw how Patty's careless behavior affected Marlowe directly.

"I'm sorry she couldn't be more understanding."

"It's dumb of me. To keep wanting that." She glanced up from where she traced her index finger over the mattress. "For her to be different, you know."

"It's not dumb to want her support."

"Yeah, but after proving over and over she's not capable of giving it, it is dumb to keep getting disappointed over it."

She'd slipped into a robe before leaving the bedroom and he was able to lean forward to tug on the oversize sleeve, pulling her down on the bed. He used her forward momentum to gather her up in his arms, pulling her so her back lay flush against his chest, his lips pressed to her ear. "I'm sorry she can't be who you need her to be."

Marlowe twisted in his arms, turning so she could look up at him. "I'm glad you can be." She pressed a firm kiss to his lips before laying a hand against his cheek. "Thank you."

"You're welcome."

They stayed like that for a long time, wrapped up in each other. And when they finally got out of bed and got ready for what would undoubtedly be a long day ahead, it was with the mutual encouragement and support formed in that quiet together.

Wyatt walked Arlo through the details he'd found on Nightwatch, now expanded with the information Michael and Anderson had shared about the two men who ran the club. Arlo made various notes, adding them to their case board as they talked through implications and the additional runs they'd make through the case files from that time.

Once they'd agreed on next steps, divvying up the work since Wyatt was still off the dive list, he focused on the day before. As he gave Arlo a full debrief on the visit to the prison, Michael's death and what information they had on the dead guard, Arlo outlined his theories.

"The guard's the inside man, putting you, Marlowe and Michael into position, but it's the hired muscle who made the hit."

"I'll bet you he's the same guy who attacked me on the Hudson River dive."

He still hadn't fully gotten over the fact that the jerk had gotten the jump on him under water, but he kept consoling himself with the knowledge that they were dealing with someone who was likely ex-military and trained with an exceptional set of skills.

"That's a sucker bet, Trumball. No way I'm taking that one." Arlo scratched a quick note in dry erase marker beneath the section of the board labeled 1995. "You run the Nightwatch crew? Any kids?"

Wyatt flipped through the file, reviewing the list of facts about the business partners who'd owned the club. "No male children. No obvious connections to the military, either."

"You think the killer's a merc?"

"Working theory only. Captain's put some feelers in with the Feds. Between the attack on my dive and the ambush at the prison if there's a line to tug there Dwayne will find it."

Arlo eyed the various photos of evidence they had up on the case board in one of the small precinct conference rooms. "If the captain's willingly introducing federal support into this it means a heck of a lot."

"Especially since he managed to hold them off when the fourth safe was recovered. If there'd been a bomb in there they'd have taken this case over."

"Let 'em." Arlo tapped a beat on his thigh with his fingers, a tune only he could hear. "Besides, I never fully understand the territorial fights over jurisdiction, anyway. Isn't keeping the city safe the real point of it all?"

Since that's the same philosophy Dwayne led his department with, Wyatt could only agree.

"So that's what I've got." Wyatt stepped back from the board and sat on the edge of the conference table, crossing his arms. "It's more than we had even yesterday, but it feels empty, too. Way too many holes still to plug to get this handled."

Wyatt studied the board, one of those holes suddenly staring at him in glaring neon. "The dive. The bastard who attacked me. How'd he know where we'd be?"

"I hate to break it to you, buddy, but you get taken out on the water with a bit of fanfare, between the police boat and the Zodiac that drops your crazy ass over and into the water."

His willingness to go that far beneath the water had always been a point of humor in their friendship, especially since Arlo had said on several occasions there was no way he'd ever put on scuba gear and drop below the water like that, even in the gleaming waters of the Caribbean instead of the murky waters of New York Harbor.

"Exactly. But whoever attacked me needed to get in position out of sight of us, which meant he had to swim to us for a bit." Wyatt shook his head, pissed he hadn't realized it from the very start. "The bastard was already in position to do that because he knew where we'd be."

Any hint of jokes had vanished as Arlo spoke. "There's only one way he knew that in advance."

"We have a leak."

He and Arlo laid it out for Dwayne in the privacy of the conference room. They'd called him in under the guise of walking him through a quick update in the case, but their captain had sensed the obvious seriousness the moment he closed the door behind them.

"These are serious charges but the implications are obvious," Dwayne said. "And it reinforces the pattern of strategically positioned insiders who gather information. The prison guard fits that, too."

"Insiders. A likely mercenary for hire. Even the heroin in the first three safes. There's a ton of upfront investment here," Arlo pointed out. "This isn't about a nightclub that closed nearly thirty years ago. I don't think it's even about Anderson or Michael McCoy. Not at its heart."

Wyatt had filled Arlo in on Marlowe's grandfather's role in looking the other way and Dwayne had confirmed when he'd come into the conference room that he'd already met with Anderson and had begun proper procedures with Internal Affairs.

Once again, the heavy weight that sat on his captain's shoulders was borne with grace and a stoic belief in doing the job.

And remained the inspiration for Wyatt of what made up the very fabric of the 86th.

"Let me handle the review of the logs from the other day." Dwayne's dark gaze roamed over the board before turning back to Wyatt and Arlo. "It looks like I'm opening a second discussion with I.A."

Marlowe wanted to call her grandfather, but she settled for a text message after she got into her office, checking in to see how he was. He'd texted quickly back that he'd call her later. Since she'd gotten a response at all she took that as a positive sign, but recognized an intentional vagueness there, too.

And also recognized she needed to give him some space.

There was a new software patch she'd been sent that she could test on one of the prototypes. She'd downloaded the details but had only half-heartedly played with the locking mechanism before giving up.

The work needed focus and hers was scattered and jumpy, bouncing from mental squirrel to squirrel.

Her father, grandfather and mother had taken top spots in her mind, yet each time those thoughts got too overwhelming, she was rewarded with the delicious memories of making love with Wyatt and the ire and frustration faded for a bit.

Those lovely memories kept her company as she shifted gears to doing mindless paperwork and she tried to stay in that happier space in her mind instead of the dour thoughts her parents seemed so adept at spinning up.

As she worked through her invoicing software, she did have an additional moment of happiness when she realized just how strong a summer she had. There were only a few days left in September but based on the last few invoices she was loading in, it appeared she'd beaten her third quarter projections by nearly 20 percent.

"Hot damn, girl. You've earned yourself a fresh cup of coffee."

She crossed to the single-cup brewer she kept in her office and started fixing a fresh mug when her gaze alighted on the map of Brooklyn she kept tacked over the wall. She'd always acknowledged her workspace had the appearance of a local entrepreneur's business and a villain's lair, with maps, safe designs and lock schematics intertwined with a print from the Brooklyn Botanic Gardens and a movie poster for *Moonstruck*.

The space was uniquely hers and she loved it, but it certainly was far from a cubicle in a high-rise or even the communal bullpen feel of the 86th.

But definitely hers.

Her gaze alighted on that movie poster once more and she envisioned some of the key scenes of the film, nearly all shot in Brooklyn Heights. Images of the water and the Manhattan skyline set the backdrop for several of those water shots and Marlowe could picture them clearly in her mind. In fact, she mused, she and Wyatt should change up their running routine and consider a run along the water, curving around Brooklyn before stopping for breakfast in Brooklyn Heights.

Maybe that weekend.

It felt good to make plans, she thought as she doctored her coffee.

Even better to think about making them with Wyatt.

As she took a sip of her coffee the real implications hit her.

Weekend plans. A slate of activities. All with Wyatt taking center stage.

Quite beyond her imaginings, Wyatt had become a part of her life. An active part, where she planned time with him and saw him in her life.

It had been a long time since she'd been in a relationship that felt this settled so soon. In fact, the more she considered it, Marlowe had to admit, it had been a long time since she'd felt settled at all, in or out of a relationship.

Yet Wyatt Trumball had changed that. With his twinkling eyes and steady attitude and that enticing mix of serious and fun, he'd snuck beneath her defenses.

And she loved him.

The weight of that stilled her and she set her mug down with a hard thud on the counter.

Love?

Unbidden, her mother's wailing that morning over how much she'd loved Marlowe's father filled her mind. The overdramatic crescendo of how much he'd hurt her yet how devastated she was that he was gone. The lifetime of love they'd shared, even though they'd spent the past two decades apart.

Marlowe had refrained from mentioning that Patty could have made a visit of her own up to the prison whenever she'd wanted. And, as she'd told Wyatt, she'd also avoided bringing up Brock because whatever happiness new love had brought into her mother's life was no match for the tragic heroine she now saw herself as the ex-wife—ex-widow?—of a brutally murdered man.

God, could it be more complex? And a little sordid, too, she admitted to herself.

This is what she came from. This was the emotional maturity of half her DNA. Was she doomed for a lifetime of the same?

It had been a fear, albeit a subtle one, she'd carried for years. But now that she was here—now that she could look to Wyatt and see someone she wanted to share her life with—she recognized those fears were unfounded.

More settled then she could have imagined, she snagged her mug and went back to her desk, determined to power through her paperwork before heading home and reveling in the success of beating her quarterly projections by 20 percent. She'd stop at the market and pick up some things for the dinner she was going to cook Wyatt. And she'd swing by to see her grandfather, determined to assure him that he would get through this time.

She'd make sure of it.

With her accounting software open, she flipped through the work she'd done over the past two weeks and began the process of inputting itemizations for invoicing. Her gaze alighted on the address on Water Street, and she remembered the job she'd done in downtown Sunset Bay last week. The large warehouse renovation that needed interior and exterior locks installed as the final piece of the renovation.

She hadn't realized it then, but that warehouse was close to the old location of Nightwatch.

Her gaze caught on the map once more and she crossed back to look at it, her mind sifting through the various buildings on that stretch of blocks. The waterfront area had been rejuvenated over the past five years, young money coming into the area giving so many places a real shot at business.

She and Wyatt had gone to Baker's Pub, one of the bars benefitting from that renaissance.

The client she was billing had renovated a warehouse into a funky mixed-use set of apartments and retail.

But a small string of warehouses remained that appeared abandoned yet maintained just to the point of not being eyesores.

Was someone just waiting on the area's value going up enough to sell them at an even higher profit? Or was it something more? Was it possible Harry Kisco and Mark Stone still owned the space?

She'd gone off half-cocked with the internet search and wouldn't do that again to Wyatt. But she couldn't deny she was curious.

Glancing down at her watch, she considered what she knew about the area. It was the middle of the day and all of those shops and restaurants did a brisk business at lunch.

What's the worst that could happen?

Someone noticed her?

If it was still Harry and Mark's domain then, surprise, surprise, they were already well aware of who she was.

And if it was owned by someone else, she'd say she was being nosy and move on.

Win-win.

Besides, if she went she could take a look around and didn't need a warrant to do it. Wyatt wouldn't have the same leeway.

A ridiculous notion, but the sense memory of holding her hand against her father's chest, trying to stop the bleeding, left an awfully big incentive to try.

Picking up her bag of tools, she dug in for a few items. She'd stow the bag in the car but she did pull out a few picks to tuck away in her pocket. Snagging her phone, she made the call to Wyatt, not surprised when she got his voice mail.

"Wyatt, it's Marlowe. I had an idea and I'm headed down to the waterfront to nose around some of those warehouses. Call me back and meet me at Baker's for lunch and I can fill you in on whether or not I see anything."

She disconnected and grimaced at the excessively cheerful tone, especially because she recognized he wasn't likely going to be happy with her decision.

But seriously, what was going to happen in the middle of the day?

With that in the forefront of her mind she headed out and navigated through Sunset Bay down to the waterfront. She managed to snag street parking and even left her bag of tools stowed on the floor of the front seat as an incentive not to linger. Anything visible through the windows of the car was fair game and she didn't want to lose them.

The warehouses matched the mental map she'd drawn of the south end of Water Street and she had to admit as she walked up to the doors that the location would have been fantastic for a nightclub. The proximity to the water and the location at the end of the main shopping thoroughfare would have drawn crowds. Young happy crowds who wanted to drink and party and enjoy themselves.

The warehouse was dark and the windows had a grimy film on them that made it hard to see anything. She pulled out her phone and took a few pictures before shoving it into her back pocket. But as she moved down the length of the building she saw a small patch visible through the window and realized she'd hit a dead end.

A long row of what looked like industrial machines

filled the space. Vaguely, she remembered these warehouses had also housed a variety of businesses through the years, from bottling for a brewery to a high-end paper factory to a small firm that made cocktail additions like jarred onions and cherries.

Whatever she thought she'd find, this obviously wasn't used by a group of thugs any longer. It didn't look like it had manufactured anything for a while and she cycled back through her earlier thought that the owner was likely holding on until real estate prices shot up even further.

On a resigned sigh she thought about her tools still sitting in the front seat and high-tailed it back to her car. She pulled out her phone, but still no message from Wyatt. With quick fingers, she tapped out a text and hit Send, just as she came up on her car.

Still up for lunch? Warehouse is a dead end. Going to do a bit of shopping on Water Street. If I don't hear from you by one, come over later for dinner.

She toyed with adding a heart emoji and stopped herself. In love or not, she wasn't quite ready to start adding emotional nuances to her texts.

Since she wasn't sure if she should be amused or irritated for giving emojis a single bit of headspace, she shoved the phone back into her pocket.

Don't overthink it, McCoy.

Unlocking the car, she pulled her tools from the front seat and popped the trunk, determined to stow her things before killing some time in the shops. If she didn't hear from him in a half hour, she'd keep to her original plan and visit her grandfather and then get the groceries for dinner.

Musing about love and emojis and what she was going to cook for dinner occupied her thoughts when she felt a large presence at her back, the distinct press of something sharp and painful against her lower back.

"Don't make a sound."

Adrenaline beat hard in her chest and, knife or not, she was city-bred and staying quiet on the orders of a criminal wasn't in her makeup. A hard stomp on his foot gave minimal satisfaction just as she felt a distinct prick at the back of her neck.

All before the world went black.

Chapter 17

Wyatt blew out a hard breath as he walked back to his desk. The morning had been difficult, but Dwayne had lived up to his reputation as a fair lawman and an equal proponent of swift action.

Callie Dumbrowski, a low-level administrator, had been called into a conference room with Captain Reed and Internal Affairs and in a matter of minutes, had disintegrated into a pile of tears over her sick child and her louse of an ex-husband who kept missing his support payments and the large payoffs she'd received for sharing specific information to a nameless, faceless buyer.

Wyatt and Arlo had watched from the other side of the one-way mirror in the interrogation room and both had remained quiet, lost in their thoughts. Although he couldn't speak for his friend, his own thoughts had been mired in questions.

Was Callie all that different from Anderson? Their balance of power and influence in the NYPD was different, of course, but the underlying reasons for their actions were the same.

Humans backed into a corner, desperate to fix something they felt powerless against.

It was the real sadness of his job and one he had never fully reconciled in his mind. While they regularly put away hardened criminals who had made their choices for nothing but ill-gotten rewards, it was easy to forget just how often they also put away people who were simply desperate and misguided.

And who somehow thought making a bad decision would miraculously fix a bad problem.

It still haunted him as he pulled his phone out of his pocket and sat down at his desk. The face lit up at the movement and he remembered he'd had a text from Marlowe about lunch that he'd glanced at and put away to look at later.

He opened the phone, only to realize he'd had a call from her, as well. He read the text first, intending to tell her he'd meet her later when he saw there'd been more to the message than the portion about lunch that had shown up on the face of his phone.

Still up for lunch? Warehouse is a dead end. Going to do a bit of shopping on Water Street. If I don't hear from you by one, come over later for dinner.

Warehouse?

The time in the upper corner of the phone was just after one so he'd missed lunch, but what was this about a warehouse? He listened to her voice mail and all that seething frustration he'd walked back to his desk with exploded.

"Damn it!"

"Trumball?" Arlo glanced over from his desk.

"I don't believe it."

He updated his partner as he called Marlowe, frustrated when her phone went to voice mail.

"Marlowe, it's me. Call me as soon as you can. What are you doing nosing around where you don't belong?"

He hung up and added a text to call him back for good measure, especially if she hadn't heard her phone ring inside a store.

Arlo settled himself in the chair beside Wyatt's desk. "You need to let her know this isn't okay."

"Hell if I don't know that?" He ran a hand through his hair, tugging hard on the ends. "What in God's name was she thinking?"

"That she knows this neighborhood and this town and it's the middle of the afternoon."

Arlo might have a point, but her actions still stuck a hard landing. And while he was happy she hadn't found anything, what if she had? What if something had happened? He and Arlo had already run the ownership for warehouses along the water and nothing had turned up so he admitted there was little risk to her, but still.

The fact that she'd put on that bright, chirpy voice and let him know what she was doing, like it was freaking okay, pissed him off.

Hadn't they gotten anywhere since her internet dive into her father's known associates?

Or was she somehow dismissing the seriousness of what was going on and the still-real risks to her own safety?

That last thought sat uncomfortably on his shoulders. Especially since he hadn't gotten a text back.

"What's the matter?"

"She hasn't texted back."

"It's not telepathy, Wyatt. Give her a minute."

"No." He shook his head, suddenly not comfortable. "I'm going to run down there."

Arlo stood. "Then I'm going with you. And when she texts before we're out of the parking lot you can keep on driving and buy me lunch instead."

Marlowe came awake on the raw, pounding headache centered in the middle of her forehead. For the briefest moment, intense pain was all she could feel, until her mind quickly cleared with the broader implications.

What had happened? Where was she?

She sat up with a start, realizing immediately she was chained to a chair bolted to the floor. She had full movement in her hands but a shackle was attached to her ankle.

Panic hit hard in her chest, cratering in her stomach as she looked around. The space was empty, even more, just sort of blank. Other than the chair she sat in, she could see a toilet in the corner and a small sink that stuck out of the wall beside it.

This was clearly a place to hold someone because

there wasn't a thing present that could do damage. There was barely anything here at all.

She cycled through what she could remember—the drive to Water Street and her intention to check out the old warehouses.

But she'd done that and hadn't found anything.

Right?

Questions still swirled through her mind, layering over that pounding headache, as she reached down to examine the lock on the ankle restraint. It was standard, but solid, and she had little ability to do anything to it with nothing but her fingers.

Wait—

She reached behind herself and felt the lock picks she'd stowed in her back pocket. She nearly retrieved one when she heard something outside the door. Shoving the pick back down in her pocket, she sat up and waited.

And watched as three men filed into the room. Two older men who looked similar in age to her father and a thicker, younger man with an impressive physique.

"Miss McCoy."

She considered how to play this and quickly determined playing dumb was not going to work in her favor.

"Let me guess. Harry, Mark and the man who killed my father."

One of the older men smiled, clearly pleased with her remarks, while the other one looked distinctly uncomfortable. The killer remained stoic, his hands behind his back as he stood in military stance.

Wyatt zeroed in ex-military, she thought as she considered the younger man. The idea fit.

"I should congratulate you then. You guessed right."

"What is this about?" she pressed.

"And why would we tell you that?"

"You kidnapped me and tied me up. What do you have to lose?"

"Oh, sweet thing, it's not that easy," the older man—the talker—said. "I hate to disappoint you, but this isn't going to be some big reveal party."

"Then tell me one thing. Why did you kill my father?"

The talker shrugged. "Loose end."

Whatever she expected, something hit with swift and furious fists at the casual response. Nay, at the dismissive response.

"You bastard."

He looked unaffected by her words, the insult flying off him like bullets against a tank.

"I've made my life as one and I'm good at it. Remember that, girlie."

The three of them disappeared as quickly as they showed up, but not before the young guy tossed a deli bag at her feet. After they were gone, she dug in to find a bottled water, sandwich and chips in the bottom.

The thought of food turned her stomach, the headache still so intense she was slightly nauseous, but she needed the food, too. Although their menacing routine had seemed cold and clearly designed so that she didn't get any ideas, she wasn't sure what their plan was.

Were they going to kill her?

A hard shudder flowed through her at that thought, the first time it truly settled in that she wasn't just in danger but in a situation she wasn't getting out of.

But why feed her?

As she cracked the tube of water, she had a second thought.

These men had proven themselves capable of the darkest of deeds. What if she was just bait for something far worse?

"Why the hell did you take her?" Mark whirled on Steve the moment they got into the office.

The ex-SEAL shrugged, clearly unconcerned by the outburst. "She was nosing around. You already said you wanted to figure out a way to use her. I figured out a way."

"She was nosing around a piece of property we don't even own anymore!" Mark exploded.

Dutch watched the exchange carefully, even as he projected a casual demeanor as he kept his gaze on his laptop.

Steve had gotten cocky, his success on the Hudson dive as well as the two kills yesterday clearly motivating him to act on impulse. Dutch had worried they had given him too much autonomy, especially as they took advantage of his varied skills. He'd done the dives independently, burying the last safe as well as trying to take out Wyatt Trumball, carrying out Dutch's plans for both. And then he'd managed the sniper kills with perfect execution.

They needed him, but it also meant they had to deal with his increasing interest in directing the work.

"She's a loose end." Steve ignored Mark's ire. "Don't worry, I'll handle her. You don't have to get your hands dirty."

"Handle her? How many people are you planning to handle before someone gets wise? The cops aren't going to rest until they figure out what happened yesterday."

"You said you wanted McCoy out of the picture. I did that."

Although Dutch appreciated the proactive nature of Steve's work, the reality was he wasn't empowered to direct anything. He was hired muscle, nothing more.

Without checking the impulse, Dutch dragged a gun out of his desk drawer. Mark's fury had provided inadvertent cover and Steve sensed the aim of the gun a fraction of a heartbeat too late. His hand had just reached his own gun, tucked in his waistband, when Dutch's shot landed true, dead center of his chest.

It was clean and fast and Dutch watched Mark take a few steps back, his throat working around swallow after swallow as he stared down at Steve's body.

"What the hell are we going to do with him?"

"Same thing we've done up to now. We'll pay to have it handled."

Because for all his ambition and all his understanding of the big scores that still awaited them, Dutch had also figured out something else as he headed toward seventy.

New York was his oyster. And with the proper cash incentive, you really could pay for anything.

Wyatt scanned the street as he drove down Water Street. The lunchtime crowd flowed in and out of restaurants and shops, a thriving, busy area.

Was he overreacting?

Would they find her in a shop or maybe having lunch by herself on a patio?

Marlowe had texted that she'd found nothing at the warehouse and was heading into the shops. And he'd be fine with that outcome.

Thrilled.

Even if he was still going to give her hell for thinking she needed to go check out anything.

But in the end, all he wanted was for her to be safe.

"There!" He pointed to the sedan at the end of the street. "That's her car."

He pulled up alongside and got out, scanning the car but assured by the fact that everything looked good. Confused, then, that she hadn't called him back, he dialed her again, trying to figure out where she was.

And heard the distinct notes of her cell phone peal from the inside of her trunk.

Marlowe felt the last bit of the lock's resistance give way under the pressure of her pick, the shackle springing open on her ankle. Although it hadn't hurt where it fitted around her body, she breathed her first easy breath at the physical freedom.

Now to deal with the door.

Although she'd hated the shackle, the chain had given her full range of motion around the room and she'd been able to examine the door before settling in to pick open the thick cuff. From what she could see, her picks weren't going to work from the inside, so she'd considered a few different courses of action on the door. She could try to use the end of the pick to jiggle the lock from the split between the door and the frame, or she could lay in wait with and use the strength of the shackle chain as a garrote, catching whoever came in unawares.

She might have a chance against the two older men, but the younger guy would flick her off like a gnat.

Which meant she had to try working the door.

Although heavy, she kept the chain wrapped in her fist, wanting to have the weapon close at hand if someone entered. Satisfied she could, at minimum, swing out with it if cornered, she bent over and went to work on the door.

And heard the distinct pop of a gunshot echo from somewhere on the other side.

Arlo was already running another set of ownership files on all the surrounding buildings as Wyatt moved around the building that had been the historic location of Nightwatch. The warehouse was truly abandoned, the grimy windows and discarded machines from whatever had come there after it had been a nightclub a testament to the passage of time and disuse.

So where was she?

There was no way she'd left her phone in the trunk and it gave him the worst sense something was wrong, even as he couldn't understand where she could be.

Arlo came up beside him, also peering in the windows in curiosity. "Nothing's flagging on these buildings."

"And we already checked and Harry Kisco and Mark Stone are no longer the owners of this building."

"They haven't been for a long time, nor were they listed as owners on anything else around here."

Wyatt slammed a hand on the window, the motion rattling the old, worn glass.

Damn it, focus.

Stilling his racing thoughts, Wyatt tried to puzzle together what had happened.

She'd parked her car and walked over here, which was about a hundred and fifty yards. He had the time stamp from his text of when she'd walked away and the phone was now in the trunk, which meant something must have happened around the car.

The car.

"Arlo! She has to be close. If someone has her, they had to drag her somewhere close. You can't just drag a woman blocks and blocks in the middle of lunch."

In unison, the two of them worked the perimeter of the warehouse, coming around to the back side, which faced away from Water Street. The distinct sounds of the ocean lapping against the boat docks that dotted the perimeter of the shoreline echoed in the afternoon breeze but not much else.

It was only as he turned from facing the water and to the back of the warehouse that Wyatt saw it.

"There. Where does that old path go?"

He and Arlo headed toward the path and noticed it took a sharp curve, the ground following the natural ebbs and flows of the shoreline.

They came to a stop when they saw a small outbuilding, about fifty yards farther down the shoreline.

Marlowe refused to waste any time. The lock wasn't easy but she knew enough about its internal mechanism to use the end of her pick as leverage, finally jiggling the door loose. Carefully, she pulled the door open, peaking to the outside as soon as she had a wedge of space to see through.

The outer room wasn't that large, but she didn't see the men, either. Without waiting another moment she took off, racing for the door visible on the far side of the space. She had no idea where she was but saw bright light shining through the windows along with that subtle scent of brine and dead fish that spoke of the shore.

She couldn't be that far from Sunset Bay. And all she needed was to get to someone who could help her and she could get to Wyatt.

The door was nearly in sight when she heard a heavy shout. Without turning around, she kept on toward her goal. Falling against it, she dragged on the doorknob, struggling to turn it in her hand, the metal knob slipping in her grip.

On a hard, anguished scream she doubled down, wrenching at the knob and getting it to turn, opening the heavy door.

Bright sunlight greeted her and she felt grasping fingers against the back of her shirt, but pushed on, racing outside.

More of that salty, slightly fetid air greeted her and she took great gulps as she raced toward the water. Gulls screamed in the air, a match for her shouts for help.

She came around a twist in the land and saw Wyatt and Arlo in the distance.

"Wyatt!"

She screamed his name just as shots rang out in the air behind her.

* * *

Wyatt raced toward Marlowe, yelling for her to get down as he saw the men in the distance behind her.

Reaching for his side arm, he and Arlo crouched in unison, warning the shooter to drop his weapon before they both let off shots.

Marlowe had already dropped to the ground, her hands over her ears, as he and Arlo went to work. Two men had been in pursuit, one of whom had immediately lifted his hands in the air.

The other got off one more shot before he was hit in the shoulder, dropping his weapon and falling down.

He and Arlo sprinted to the men as Arlo called in for backup. Wyatt's gaze tracked on Marlowe as they passed her on the way toward the men.

"I'll be right back."

"Go! I'm fine but there might be a third."

Arlo nodded that he'd also heard about a third and they reached the men, subduing them.

"Where's your buddy?" Wyatt screamed out the request as he pressed the uninjured man to the ground, his arms behind his back.

"He's dead."

The man's voice was dull, his eyes empty, and while Wyatt wouldn't believe anything until the scene was cleared, that lack of reaction helped calm his adrenaline slightly.

Because they weren't far from Water Street, two cops on patrol had already arrived, running down toward the water from the high street. Arlo hollered out the instruction to watch their back, relaying Marlowe's instructions, but the guy on the ground just kept repeating the same.

"He's dead. It's just the two of us."

It was only when further backup arrived, two officers handling the man in Wyatt's custody, that he moved inside to sweep the area.

And found a very large man, dead of a shot to the chest.

Wyatt knew they'd have answers soon, but as he stared down at that large form, he couldn't shake the sense that this was the man who'd tried to kill him beneath the waters of the Hudson.

Marlowe allowed the adrenaline coursing through her body to do its work. She'd faced enough of it over the past week to know the only thing to do was settle in and take deep breaths.

And thank her lucky stars that Wyatt and Arlo were safe and that she'd walked out alive.

A swarm of cops from the 86th had descended on the old outbuilding, processing the crime scene and asking her any number of questions. She answered them all, over and over, while waiting for Wyatt.

What had she done?

She'd blithely headed off to the warehouse, well aware it wasn't the best idea. But she'd gone anyway and she'd put Wyatt and Arlo in danger because of it.

That thought kept her steady company as she shivered under a police blanket, staring out over the water.

Captain Reed arrived in short order, immediately coming to her and taking her in his arms, holding her close. "I'd really like a day without any McCoys in it. Can you try to work on that?"

"I'd like that, Uncle D. More than I can say."

He chuckled and rubbed her back, keeping her in a tight hold as she shivered her way through tears.

"Have you seen Wyatt?" She finally got her tears under control enough to ask. "I'm sorry I put him in this position and I'd like to apologize."

"I think I'm going to have to get in line behind Trumball to kick your ass for going out on your own, but I can't argue with your results. You brought them down, Marlowe."

"Who down?" She lifted her head and found Wyatt standing just behind Dwayne.

His voice hinted at his pride in her when he finally spoke. "The masterminds behind the safes and your father's murder and, from what details we found inside, a large cache of heroin that the DEA's going out now to intercept. It's about two days south of here on a ship working its way up the Atlantic."

"That's what this was about?"

"Best we can tell," Wyatt affirmed.

"That's why he called my father a loose end."

Dwayne's eyes narrowed at that. "Which one?"

"The one who was shot. He called my father a loose end."

"We'll get to the bottom of it. The bastard is entitled to his medical treatment but the moment we're able, we're getting him in a box. In fact," Dwayne said, glancing between the two of them, "let me go see about that now."

"Wyatt, I'm so sorry."

Wyatt moved up and pulled her close, wrapping his arms around her, thick blanket and all. "I'll yell and carry on later. Right now I just want to hold you."

She wrapped her hands around his waist, holding on for all she was worth.

"Is it really over?"

"There's all that'll come next, but the danger? The safes? The threats to you and your family?" He pressed a kiss against her head. "Yes, it's over."

A long, shuddering breath fell from her lips and she hadn't realized just how hard she'd been holding it in.

Her future was in sight. A wonderful place that had been waiting for her.

Past the secrets that had lived in a warehouse in Brooklyn for nearly three decades.

Past her father's and grandfather's mistakes.

Past her own lonely past.

And Wyatt stood in that future.

"You know, I realized something earlier."

"What's that?" he whispered again against her temple.

She stared up at him. "I love you. It sort of caught me by surprise, but it's as real as I could have ever imagined."

"You know, that's funny."

"Funny?"

"Yeah, because somewhere between admiring your legs in Prospect Park and racing you through it, I fell in love with you, too."

She'd hoped.

All while she'd tried on her feelings and committed to the idea of diving in and really loving him, she'd wondered how he felt. If he cared for her and if maybe he'd catch up to her feelings at some point.

How wonderful to realize he felt them, too.

"I love you, Marlowe."

"I love you, too." She kissed him, all the promise of that glorious future rising up between them.

But when they pulled back, their gazes locked, and she knew something else. Whatever more they shared, a foundation of fun, flirty humor existed between them. With the danger pushed aside, it was time to find that sense of fun again.

The carefree ability to laugh.

"You know, you promised me something this morning and I don't want you to think I'd forgotten."

He tilted his head, clearly trying to remember what they'd discussed. "What's that?"

"Kitchen sex, Wyatt. It's poor form to tease a woman with an offer like that and not deliver."

His mouth turned down at the edges, his face set in grave lines. But the twinkle in his blue eyes didn't have her believing his act for a second.

"Well, then, I guess I'm honor bound to take you home and deliver on my promise."

She smiled up at him and knew all the love she felt shined in her eyes. "See that you do."

* * * * *

Author Note

I had so much fun writing this book. It's always amazing to me when a small news story can suddenly spark a very big idea. The book you just read was a result of a local news piece I watched on the NYPD's divers that expanded into a series in this writer's imagination.

While I've done quite a bit of research on this special branch of the NYPD, there are some aspects of the divers' work that are not widely available. I suspect this is for both their safety, as well as the city they're protecting. To that end, I've used my imagination in crafting a series around the core idea of heroes and heroines who protect the waters around New York as their life's work.

I hope you'll forgive any license I've taken in service to the story. Any errors in actual procedure are all mine.

#2243 CHASING A COLTON KILLER
The Coltons of New York
by Deborah Fletcher Mello
Stella Maxwell is one story away from Pulitzer gold, but when she becomes the prime suspect in the murder of her ex-boyfriend, those aspirations are put on hold. FBI agent Brennan Colton suspects Stella might be guilty of something, but it isn't murder. Between his concern for Stella's well-being and the notorious Landmark Killer taunting them, Brennan never anticipates fighting for his heart.

#2244 MISSING IN TEXAS
by Karen Whiddon
It's been four brutal years for Jake Cassin, who finally locates the daughter who's been missing all that time. But his little girl is abducted before he can even meet her. Despite his reservations and an unwanted stirring of attraction, he must work with Edie Beswick, her adoptive mother, who is just as frantic as he is. How can they stay rational on this desperate search when they have everything to lose?

#2245 A FIREFIGHTER'S HIDDEN TRUTH
Sierra's Web • by Tara Taylor Quinn
When Luke Dennison wakes up in the hospital with amnesia, he doesn't know why a beautiful woman is glaring down at him. He soon learns he is a firefighter, a father and someone wants them both dead. After engaging the experts of Sierra's Web, Luke and Shelby are whisked into protective custody. Could this proximity bring them to a greater understanding of each other...or finally separate them forever?

#2246 TEXAS LAW: SERIAL MANHUNT
Texas Law • by Jennifer D. Bokal
For more than twenty years, Sage Sauter has been keeping a secret—her daughter's biological father is Dr. Michael O'Brien. Michael has never forgotten about his first love, Sage. So when Sage's daughter shows up at his hospital—presumably after being attacked by a serial killer—he offers to help. Sage knows that Michael's the best forensic pathologist around, but she's terrified that he'll discover her secret if he gets involved with a very deadly investigation.

Get 3 FREE REWARDS!

We'll send you 2 FREE Books <u>plus</u> a FREE Mystery Gift.

FREE Value Over **$20**

Both the **Harlequin Intrigue®** and **Harlequin® Romantic Suspense** series feature compelling novels filled with heart-racing action-packed romance that will keep you on the edge of your seat.

HARLEQUIN
PLUS

Try the best multimedia
subscription service for romance
readers like you!

Read, Watch and Play.

Experience the easiest way to get
the romance content you crave.

Start your **FREE TRIAL** at
<u>www.harlequinplus.com/freetrial</u>.